GUARIONEX, TAINO CACIQUE: A HERO FALLS

GUARIONEX, TAINO CACIQUE: A HERO FALLS

JUANANTOÑIO

© 2016 juanantoñio
All rights reserved.

ISBN: 1539141667
ISBN 13: 9781539141662
Library of Congress Control Number: 2016916555
CreateSpace Independent Publishing Platform
North Charleston, South Carolina

PREFACE

The town in which I was born—the Land of the Sun, in the Arawak language—is in the NW section of a Caribbean island, and this area was part of Guarionex's domain. It is a small town of modest resources, except for the magnificent limestone hills and cliffs that cradle its southern end and wrap around to meet the ocean and the Atlantic shore to its north. It has always seemed a magical place. Family legend has it that the mothers of each generation come here to bathe their newborns. My mother has said she did this with me.

Millions of years ago, a volcanic eruption covered the northwest part of the island, and the volcanic streaks in the rock and the black sand mixed with the golden sand may be plainly seen. If one drills through this rocky layer, one can find the pristine primeval beach that was covered by the eruption. All mysteries have hidden layers that are beyond our sight and comprehension. What secrets were forever lost in this ancient land whose time was stopped by the explosion?

This covering of thick sandstone, towering limestone cliffs, and lava extending to the shore and beyond, beneath the roiling surf, has been carved into a phantasmagoric zoo of animals, gargoyles, Jacuzzi-like tubs of whirling water, and monsters. I have even found miniature Navajo cliff dwellings absent only the inhabitants, if one rules out the sea snails. And, I hesitate to say, I have also seen a representation of a queen with a swaddled child. At first, I was stunned. How had I, in years and countless times of walking this shore (and many generations of my family also walking this land), never heard of or seen this before? So clearly etched! Was it the work of a contemporary artisan or an undiscovered Taino artifact? Over a few days, I observed that the clarity varied with the time of day and placement of sun, clouds, and shadows. It was something only seen rarely at certain times of year or day. My psychological and psychoanalytic training came into play, and I asked myself: What about me made me search to see such a fleeting figure? To construct this out of misted air, sunlight, shadow, and rock? And so was born the story of Guarionex.

And so, I walk along the shore with the living, the dead, and ancient of flesh and fantasy. Here my stories emerge written upon the clouds. The only place where I am not capable of lying to myself. As I sit in the shadow of a cragged boulder, which in ancient times came loose from the cliff face, and look out on the ocean, watching for behemoth and its calf, I feel in the throes of the original creation. I see that the creation was not an act but a continuing work in this world. And I feel the presence of Guarionex. I feel his stride, the wind on his naked body, the sun's heat, and his love for Star of the Sea. And I hear the songs of Star of the Sea and her love and courage in leading the way along the journey. And I hear a voice, a humble scribe, his words describing what he has seen and heard as he accompanied Guarionex, and that he writes these words that I may pass them on.

juanantoñio

PROLOGUE

Knowing
Lepidus says of Antony:
"There are not evils enough
to darken all his goodness"

Antony, hearing of Cleopatra's
Death, exclaims,
My thoughts, life, and flesh
But vessels for things
Not understood.
In good what hell
Unleashed?
In evil deeds what good
Released?

Kicked, pushed aside
Nurtured on bitterness
Ambition defeating neglect
Thirst slaked by my own tears
Cruelty, revenge on others
Tasted sweet, moist and sweet,
Upraised on wings of self
I walked tall on evil deeds

Cruelty served with soft, open hands
Punishing burdens dispersed
As a fleeing flock of colored birds
Cruising as gorging leviathan
Releasing treasured nutrient
For those below
Breaching with mighty spouts
Creating fullness and the world
A leap and splash
A splendid passage
Life the water
My breath divinity
Touched by the eternal
With every life I took.

BOOK 1

A HERO FALLS:
GUARIONEX, BRAVE NOBLE LORD,
THE LAST OF HIS NAME

THE HUMBLE SCRIBE RETURNS
Do not despair,
This time the last, to tell a tale
Of gods and demigods

As I am called to further isles of
Humanity far from where your
Dreams or thoughts reside
Your humble scribe now kindly turned
As he is loosed from the tortured
Ways of your dream-destinies sees clearly
The sufferings of your mortal flesh
And attempts to paper the void
That on every side extends.

Your fantasies of dancing gods
Benign goals and ends overpowering
The surrounding dark and cold
Awaken pity and paternal concern

GUARIONEX, THE LAST OF HIS NAME, SPEAKS OF IMPENDING DEATH
The full white birds by wind impelled
That sailed to my island home
Where the sun is born
And returns to rest at end of day,
The land of the beauteous sun
Where my clan walked in the
Cupped hands of many gods,
Came to take me, Cacique Father,
To find the land where the earth
Spills the mother waters of eternity

And washes out shining stones
Of every color of the flowers of the field

I stood sailing on currents of wind and sea
At the judgment of the lowest born
Who, seeing paradise, sought gold
Wealth and eternal life,
Which even the gods who
Are so "blessed" despise.
Gold but mortality's residue,
Only the One Supreme moves
With fullness in eternity

My land out of sight a full day and night
Tended fire pit on the ship's prow burning
To consume my flesh if direction
I did not give to please their greed.
It was then I embraced the fire
Rather than bring their misery
To unsullied lands

GUARIONEX'S LAST WORDS BEFORE BOARDING THE SHIPS
I see the dark and light of the mountains
Beyond the beating wings
Of my words, the bursting color hue of
The sea's profoundest depths
Profess my love for you
And my ancient home

I trill untiringly in the birds'
Ringing notes of loneliness

That shatter each day's
Connection to the next

I grind the rocks with wrath
And mix a slurry soup of tears and sea
To drink and shape my ancestors' progeny,
To compose my words, limbs and thoughts

I see my destiny clear from the first day
Of creation to now and beyond.
The world throbs with clarity
As it dissolves, a dream

I now recall I had forgotten all
And am yet to complete the great
Circle of my destiny and will return
As the One Supreme recalls my name

GUARIONEX IN THE FIRE
I am the flaming shaft
Released to strike
The fullest freedom where
Self dissolves to soul
And desire creates the world
Receding to a sphere of
Eternal nothingness

THE HUMBLE SCRIBE IN GRIEF REPORTS
He rose a spark, smoke
On hot currents twisting
In an upward dance,

And from that distance
Bound by ties of love
He recalled and saw all that
He ever was and would be,
Every step and fall

His soul now free from
Flesh's burden was shaped
By dry winds and wet
By river spouts
Spilled liquid blessings
That contoured his
Spirit, soul, and mind

He heard a metered beat
As a heart made of
Dragonfly wings would beat,
Pulsing to eternity's flow
One beat to a galaxy's turn
All of humanity's
Sufferings and passions
Misplaced on dreams of flesh,
Blinded by solidity, form and shape
And he saw near and far
Big and small, to the
Beginning and the end
Increase and decrease
And saw that all was but
The shadow of the One Supreme

Rains fell, hot winds scoured his soul,
Flattened, molded, smoothed its contours

Whole mountain ranges slipped and slid
To materiality turning to ego, self,
Desire and rapacious wakefulness
Dark things took root
Surged upward as in search of sun
That turned gold, then black,
Red and green in turn
Gave fruit, seeds dispersed,
Diverged and grew again
As things stranger than ever seen

Aeons of dry winds of fine-milled
Dust from scorched mountains
And alien lands cut and shaped his soul,
Serrated scapes of pockmarked
Naked rock carved to misshapen faces
Bloating from internal heat,
Cracking even the marble of his soul,
Veins of stress, turning to dust,
Melting symmetry, leaving as detritus
What took infinity to build

And then his life and fate unfolded
And evanesced as in a dream

GUARIONEX, THE LAST OF HIS NAME, IN DEATH, REMEMBERS HIS INFANCY

Crossing the great waters,
A severed yearning and
An uncanny spirit of misery
Drive me to self's creation

Embraced by a present wind,
Salt spray of an opaque sea
To never need an other
To summon the magic of the world
For loving ministrations to me

The clan had set upon the sea
Hunted by the fierce Carib
From pearled green isle to isle,
From one to other pearled green purchase
This crossing a storm beset the boat
And sudden wave from mother's arms
Washed the infant boy away
Upon undulating waves

Soon out of reach and sight
Floating dry as an autumn leaf
On a sun-scoured promontory,
Upheld on a lady's arm
Woman of the sea intent on charity
A manatee, a mermaid of old,
A woman dressed in flowing robes,
All these tales were told
A creature dry, untouched by waters
Yet part of them, on, above, below
Breaching spouting leaping
In joyful bounds, receding
To never be seen again

I remember a joyful voice with
Nature's music of calming winds,
The shore's susurrations, the birds'
Morning call, the presence of the sun's

Sweet caress of heat, the moon's silent call
All turned to words, which sounded and taught
Their meaning inside of me though I had not
Yet learned to speak
Guarionex would
Tell me with wonder in his eyes,
Many years later, from that first
Moment he could speak and
Understand the birds of the air
And the fish of the sea,
And all the creatures of the land,
Water and sky that accompany them,
And that is why he never uttered word
Or sign to man or woman
Until he became a man.
All the creatures
Taught him the world and value of things
And he had no time for the teachings of the clan
It was this that he taught the clan when
First he spoke

Guarionex had no words for what he saw
Arawak falls short (as does your tongue,
Poor reader, living in a reality
Of light-filled boxes)
Guarionex took as words and thoughts
All that moves and sings, all the shapes,
Colors, seeing, buried, flying things
And forms that glorify this world by
The Words and Thoughts of the One Supreme

Guarionex spoke in signs
And calls of all the creatures,

Of the birds that daily visited
The shore and the embracing sea
Their habits of skimming the sea,
Floating therein, or in swimming
Currents of air and water,
Flocking and spreading to the sky
And beyond
High, low, on the horizon
Of sky and sea, or to the mountains
And rocky lairs or the
Trees that sing with the voices of many gods
Where they gather to pass the night
And if in these words is not enough
And language fails then add
The fish of the sea, their numbers
And variety, all the ways of carrying young
And knowledge of reef and deep
Their bright colors, one handful
Of which would do proud for all
The regiments of humankind's militaries
And all their nations' flags
And the mollusks and the squids
All the ways to crawl with
Their hand-signing possibilities
And the creatures of forest and plain
Their shape, colors and forms
Their prancing, leaping and
Many-shaped brayings and roars
The care of their young, their vigilance of
Readiness and truth to their own kind
And the toiling insects, upon whose small backs
We stand while they work to replenish and

Repair the Earth, bring back to nature what is hers
(What rises decays to rise in form again
Your shape, your form, dear reader)
And flower the plains with all that grows
And the green grasses of sea and land
And the fruits with their free bounty
Which maintain all that walks and swims and flies
And the invisible world of beings that swarm all things
A shield against want and disease
That cover us in greater numbers than all our cells
(O, proud reader, how mighty, free, invincible you stand
Ruler of the universe on a pinnacle
Built of the works and deeds of your
Most humble kin)

The truth, signs and sounds of all of these
Were seen and heard by Guarionex
When as infant, the charity of
The lady of the sea saved him.

He spoke with his dance,
I struggled to understand
Where walked his clan
The land of the sun it was called
The portal of the sun from where it flew
Each day to the westerly world

Guarionex danced and
With signs and sounds and
Drawings in the sand, fashioned
By a sharpened shell,
And leaps and bounds,

Which spread the sand to mirror the world,
Guarionex sang as birds at dawn
And night each singing to
Its own kind in different trills.
As the snake crawls, he walked
And as the tortoise swims with elegant ease
Transforming to lumbering awkward,
In all its forms Guarionex spoke
With all the signs and sounds
Of all the creatures one sees and hears
Even those of the darkest nights
But overriding all of these his stately posture,
Posturing and bodily grace
Sable-skinned lord and king
By birth, deed and temperament
And heavenly blessing
In serene and prayerful contemplation
And adoration of all nature
And of the One Supreme
Even in the leaps and bounds
And pirouettes, as he told of
What he dreamt, on that
Fateful crossing to the land
Of the beauteous sun
Slowly conveyed to me,
With the passage of days and moons
I understood
In the language of nature
And now I put it down in
Humankind's tongue that falls
Short due to my incapacities

The geologic record will confirm
Though not currently, due to science's
Primitivity, all that follows as the history
Of life on Earth, and will explain many
Anomalies now extant

ADDENDUM TO HISTORY OF THE EARTH AS TOLD TO THE HUMBLE SCRIBE BY GUARIONEX, THE LAST OF HIS NAME

There was a time before this time
In which each creature in turn
Ruled the Earth and lifted great cities
Of their own kind and enterprise that
Penetrated even the darkest recesses
Of the heavens even to the stars

Leviathan did
In mighty strides upon the Earth
Build great cities, now
Fallen of their own weight
Into themselves and remain as the
Mountain ranges that gird the Earth

And the fish, in alliance with
Mollusks and squids, great cities also built
With moving vehicles that traveled all
Through time, but these are
Covered now and overgrown
With living reefs, which many
Of their kind now colonize

In remembrance of greatness in all
And far-flung voyages through time
And space, but their greatest
Accomplishments were dug so deep
To bear the weight of cities
So high they scraped the sky
And it is said one could step
From the highest tower to the moon
But those are gone, for under such weight,
The mantle caved, and the Earth's core
Broke through, a ring of fire
Over half the world
The remaining clue

And the creatures of the plains and forest
Also ruled all they surveyed,
There was no ambition
They did not dare
Now all that's left of majestic
Dwellings that reached to top the sky
And spread over all the Earth
Are the trees and grasses
Mere skeletal remains of profound
Edifices that would have fed many worlds

All these had strived to challenge the One Supreme
And with each other were in constant war
The vestiges of which we see in lions
Preying on antelopes and creatures
Of the plains, and the hawk on smaller game
Your humble scribe must interject that
The roots of these and other remnant feuds

The gore-filled history upon which they rest
Are too disconcerting to tell, as the reader
Would lose all faith in the orderliness of the universe
All things heal slowly though slowly for the worse
As one fell the other rose
Enslavement followed war
Then war to repay war
Finally this led to a universal pact
Where all things of mind's devise
Rising at least from ambition
And desire's lust for gold and strength
Deteriorating to contest and violent ends
Were given up and they surrendered
To Nature's state and the watchful eye
Of the One Supreme, even as seen today

Leviathan returned to the sea
From where it had emerged
Fish retreated from the land
Except the more defiant mollusks
And crabs populating by right
Both sea and land where they converge
The sky was left to the birds,
And creatures of the forests and plains
The earth as was fit
And then in paroxysm of wisdom
Not before or since ever seen
Dominion of all was given to
The insects and invisible toilers
And the grasses for they sustained
The lives of all and order of the world
And so it is today, poor deluded reader,

Just in case you thought the world
Was yours to rule, when all you do is take
The ancestors of humankind no mind
Were given, as all agreed they would
Not amount to much and did not have to
Sign the pact, a grave mistake.

CARIDAD BRINGS THE INFANT, GUARIONEX, TO THE LAND OF THE SUN

Guarionex remembered Caridad, as this
Is what he called her, one of caridad,
Through waters, deep and dark, carrying him
To understanding.

They coursed through water as the birds
Might fly through air, or as the wind
Might do through the affairs of humankind
Sweeping aside, pushing through but
Leaving unruffled, untouched on the other side
Lifted by warm currents on outstretched wings
Falling on cold, buoyed by speed,
Effortless watery flight on inconstant beats
Sometimes roiling the undulating waves
Or below in the deep through the heart
Of an opal stone, or deeper still
In cold dark drifts of midnight sea
And at bottom dropping through pits
Shadowing deep ravines where sudden
Shapes of bulked things of many arms,
Or schools of moon-colored fish
Darting left to right, enveloping them
As remolous tides might gently grasp

And push them to their destiny, and yet
They breathed as in a dream of air beneath
The sea, and through all, big devouring small,
Small ingesting the grasses of the sea,
Large shadows fat with maw's acquest
Through the moment and noise of the sea,
Guarionex heard the lady of the sea and
How the creatures all, the fish, mammals
Birds and all, conversed with all, and
The lady of common things, what they
Would do that day and the next, where
To go and when, whether rain or sun
And argued how could fish swim and sleep
Guarionex heard them in his mind and ears
And answered them and asked where
His mother was after being untimely
Ripped from her, they could not reply,
But then said, your mother carries
You yet to your new home

And with that all the fish of all the world
Gathered here in the Caribbean Sea
Of all colors and sizes, and preyed not
On one another, arranging themselves
As the galaxies of stars, yellow fish as fiery stars
And others as fire-strings of the warp and woof
Of the universe, and dark fish as the dark vast
Spaces separating all, and spinning
Many-colored ones as kaleidoscopic nova bursts

And Guarionex, before speaking one word of
Humankind's discourse, knew in his heart
The vast expanse of reality, and that time and space

Solidity and form were but illusion of mortality
And gave it its boundaries
None of these last, but passes
Through each and then again,

In this wordless revelation, a swollen
Wave reached up as if to slap the moon
And carried lady and infant onto the shore
And she as manatee swam away
Guarionex was speaking
But suddenly changed
Some great emotion burst
As he recalled parting from Caridad,
A strange light came
Upon him and a vision that
Brought him down upon his knees
In supplication of relief
His life unfolded before his eyes,
Great suffering shook him
I set aside hammer and chisel
(Yes, dear reader, in those days
I carved my notes in stone
An arduous task you may believe)
As I approached he signaled me back
To record

BECOMING: GUARIONEX EXPLAINS
It was not the past, but what is to come
How may I set my steps through this
A distant land not yet extant
Where I am yet undreamt
Undreaming seeing but the surface of things

The plain of things, how things appear,
Sensing not the heart's constant beat
The silent beat to round embrace
Both friend and enemy
To hear humanity

The distant past I know or
Can explain, defend in argument,
The present see, feel and smell
Satisfy hunger and thirst,
But what lies ahead hear, feel nor taste
The past I may forgive infirmity
Prepare resurgency, the present
Justify by circumstance,
But the future binds me to today's
Consequential facts, failings, omissions,
Failings surpassing sufficiency to this day
How repair injuries, avoid weakness
That hides to spring well nourished,
Fully grown evil to come?

Do roots extend to water's first embrace
Or beyond to dryness to start the quest
Again? Do berries feed the roosting birds
Or hatchlings of next spring
Or perennial waves of birds and trees?
To where does good extend or evil reign?
Where do I exist, yesterday, today
Or in morrow's day?

I am the shaft finally released
From the suffering of this world
Unstoppable, striking

The fullest freedom of the self
Where self dissolves to soul.

*Your humble, derided scribe interjects
The despair of Guarionex, Brave Noble Lord,
The last of his name, resides
In that he, with his family,
Were the leading edge of his clan
About to arrive after an aeon's journey
At the promised paradise of the
Beautiful land of the sun
And though the lady's rescue
Seemed but an instant, as a
Dream's nighttime foray,
Centuries were consumed
From his being washed overboard
To his being found by Yumac
At a time his clan was already
Well established.
Yumac knew his name
And place as Guarionex,
Brave Noble Lord, but
Last of his name,
Was yet to be appended
But we have yet other tales to tell*

BOOK 2

GUARIONEX, BRAVE NOBLE LORD, THE FIRST OF THE NAME

GUARIONEX,
BRAVE NOBLE LORD,
THE FIRST OF THE NAME;
AND STAR OF THE SEA,
MOTHER OF ALL

As the creatures of the Earth returned
To nature's way, there rose another
To walk upright
They blossomed forward facing, strong,
Unbidden, unannounced, as a firefly
From an abysm may rise to a silent
Wooded dale, but answering
An unspoken word, a name
An intonation, an intention,
From forgotten beginning times,
A moving force indolent
Until brought forth by sun
And beating rain

And so were our people born
A place of seeping water dug from earth
A rivulet nursed by inconstant rain
Then joining streams to bend and drink
Led by Brave Noble Lord,
Guarionex, the first to bear the name,
And Star of the Sea,
The headwaters of the clan,
His betrothed
So did our people flow
One great stream, a river found,
A place to paddle from freedom

To resting place, a home,
The Land of the Sun

I, Guarionex, the last to bear the name,
As many names removed as
There are moons in a cacique's life
From Guarionex, the first to bear the name,
I was thrown to the sea by the winds of fate
In the great crossing of the great waters
From a place to paddle, Orinoco,
To the Land of the Sun,
And though it seemed an instant
From fall to shore's safety
Many years had passed
My name, father and mother forgotten
And the crossing of distant mention
But Yumac, the god, knew and
Called my name to destiny
The telling of the tale of Guarionex,
Brave Noble Lord, the last of his name,
His rise from infant cast upon
A tropic beach, adoption by Yumac,
And who walked as those born of gods walk,
And rise to leader of his people
And then his death and return
To strife with the ancient enemy,
Must await the telling of his people's
Story, your humble scribe regrets,
This not by my intent, but
Guarionex's elocutions

THE TALE OF GUARIONEX, THE FIRST TO BEAR THE NAME, BRAVE NOBLE LORD, AS TOLD TO THE HUMBLE SCRIBE BY GUARIONEX, THE LAST OF THE NAME

He opened first his eyes
Mountain ranges fell to dust and void
And countless times merged
As rock, world and humankind
Then past all time, word and deed
To void again unchanged
Frozen time in glacial form flowed sinking
Into cradling holes before creation
And toward its end dragging mountain boulders
Across the face of imagined history,
Deeply scarring possibility

Made of flesh and form
Toward the light he climbed,
Granite leeching into bone
His pace not measured by human span or thought
But by galaxies unhurried, birthing and dying
He climbed, each step measuring a life
A life sloughed off
To start again, a step, then death
Each death adding to the next, an endless once,
He died every man and woman
Each mite, crawling, flying, swimming thing
Each blade of grass and grain of sand
Until each step numbered countless lives
With each sloughed life, there died all things
And every word and act
Unending climb in dark

The word "light" was born
Now spoken, now called by name,
Yet again mountain ranges
Fell to dust and rose again before
He entered the Earth's domed blue sky

STAR OF THE SEA IS CALLED TO LIGHT

In the darkest water's depth
Earth's rifts spilled a flow
Of incandescent rocks
Which made her body shine
As a red dwarf pulsing star
With mouth agape against the sinuous
Current that gives nourishment to all
The gliding creatures of the dense nutrient sea

With graceful fins to maintain her place
Facing the red glowing warmth
No thought, stillness nor desire
Swallowing the swirling sea
The current's filling flow held her
Balanced between the crush and flow
All creation birthing, dying,
Born again through her
Until she craved the light
Not knowing its kind or name

Woman, your name is spoken,
All life, all seed of life has flowed through you
So you may fertilize the land
With all living things that are to come.
These words, each one a bell resounding,

Awakened some part of her
That understood and could see beyond
Could plan and master things as might a god

The ancient god who spoke these words
Loved woman more than man,
For she was more fully made in his image,
And in a fit of love for self
Gave her a fuller measure of love
Beyond all reason a strength to love
And that encompassed both life and death

But in a stronger strike of jealousy,
For her soul shone brighter still than
His own which could not love
But that which mirrored him,
He gave her pain in love
Through man's betrayal and disloyalty
And child's ingratitude
But to this god's dismay, this steeled her soul
And she rose higher still in creation's
Hierarchy of which he too was part,
In crescendos of passion he saw
That he had gone too far
Seeing his mirrored soul in her
To be more beautiful than he could aspire
Imprisoned in envy's grasp
He measured love to loss
So pain would ever equal love
Even as she gave birth to the world

All this in her ascent to water's surface calm
She escaped death that day
Because she would pay that debt in pain

In warmth of the sun after the long ascent
A yearning void split in two
The tumultuous pair of love and pain
Innocent still of joining's agony
No longer finned leviathan but of female form
Of voluptuous grace she rode
In god's cupped hand upon the waves
And landed by verdant plains alone
Where all was green and in its place
Nothing moved except the wind
No sound but the rasping blades of grass
And bristling leaves, one upon the other
In undulating waves

Fine of form *and thrice again and more*
Of voluptuous grace, for this woman
More than beautiful, shone from within,
Like the sun to the moon, and gave freely
As a summer shower to parched sands
That answering bloomed in deepest colors
Of eternal love, your ignorant
And humble loquacious scribe must speak
When woman's grace is faintly praised
With smooth brown skin bathed by the sun
And almond eyes which called forth
The fruits of this world

THE ANCIENT ONE CALLED FORTH
Both man and woman walked
Among the living and dying things,
All grass and fruit, and yet
Did not meet, for the grass recomposed
Itself on passing and they left no trace

Of their diverging paths
The ancient one had a trial for each
A service to his power and rule
Before they met

They left no trace of passing there
They felt a void and could find
No path nor one create
Passing into the time of the sun
And moon, of living things,
Of pain and loss, of death
Regret and sin, of man's
And woman's thought, deeds and words,
Which all betray

And man bitterly exclaimed:
Though now just born to light
I feel the sins of all
Unborn and yet to be
I need to be of rock and darkness hewn
To bear a weight as this, all things foreseen
Not from godly sight but felt pain and loss
What hand has torn me from the earth
And water down below?
Eternal life though in black night
Is better than quicksilver time of *soledad,*
Cursed be this tyrant god
Whose ends through my travails
And pain will be revealed
And yet the pain is small
And easily born, all loss
And pain, regret, defiance but a grain of sand

To this yearning void compared

THE ANCIENT ONE MAKES HIS PLAY
To consummate his plan
He whispered well into the ear of man
The dangers of the keepers of the winds
And the giants that guarded them
For charged and powered by the ancient one
And challenged not by beast or lesser god
They drank, ate and played
Then slept as desire swayed,
At night or day, they walked
As gods would walk
The ancient one would remove
Them all to rule the world alone
But he feared their father's fate
From whose blood they sprang,
Better that man carry the brunt
Of enmity

He said, O piteous naked man in paradise
Not you nor yours will ever rest in peace,
But work all your days to please
The keepers of the winds and their giant slaves
They will crush your first and second born
Like sparrow's eggs and suck their juices dry

This awoke in man a fiery rage
That burns unto this day, and man exclaimed:
My arm alone, my fist will rend unsafe
This world against the giants
And the keepers of the winds
I will secure the safety of my progeny
Monsters too multiply and hidden evil seed
Will rise an age distant now

But loved offspring and strong will vanquish
The evil of their days

And having said, vainglorious man sought out
The keepers of the winds and giants too
That guarded them, and slew them as they slept
He crushed their heads and sucked them dry
And was satisfied

Never had creation's plan or thought, intent,
Released a creature such as man

To their surprise and regret
The keepers of the winds that blew in orderly
Progressions from north and south
Then east and west, balancing each
Without destruction, had become too proud,
And the giants who walked
Where they pleased, now were no more

And here your ever humble and modest scribe
In apologetic style and your patient
Forbearance requesting, must interject
That man, though intentioned well to love,
Protect, secure the well-being of future humankind
Thus freed the winds to lash the Earth
With furious storms and tides, and so unbalance harmony
That lion first thought to eat the lamb
And man to thrill at killing man
It will be said in your time, dear reader,
In old Vienna, "Man is wolf to man"
And where giants walked, pestilence freed
To walk prouder still, and where it pleased,

The ancient one, the enemy, joyful that ruling
Would be eased and men would slay
In name of love, and burn their goods to him.
So love betrayed once more, man would
Remain an easy prey and slave
And is unto this day

Another task befell the female of the pair
There crept unto this land from secret plagues
Of times before, female creatures of fair design
And grace who with improvident excess
Would eat their young and careless consorts, too
The furies as they were known, and of later fame,
Reputed as from same seed of blood
As giant spawn, they had played at love
With the ancient one, for he enjoyed
Sex and blood, and would kill
In ecstasy full, a score of them
It was he who taught them well, the blood
Sport thrill, but he had wearied, and wary, too,
That provoked by greed and lesser gods,
They planned to dance upon his grave
Buried in foul excrement

Now woman, he intoned with soft whispering,
These will prey upon you, your progeny come of man,
As me they claim as god supreme and will not share
And hunt you down and take your man
To fill their appetites
How simple to provoke and take his ease
As woman, female privy to their wiles,
Could close with them and gain their trust

Wandering lost throughout the plain
With plaited vines, she captured many
Of succulent game that she had spewed
In practice run of fertility and by happenstance,
Or so she said, entered upon their camp,
Straining under cacophony of leaping, braying game,
Wild boar, hare, deer, elk and fowl

The furies, used to fruits and grain, and occasional
Lovers' or offsprings' blood, saw an abundant feast
And woman's promise of roasted meat, another first,
That would fill the nose and heart of the ancient god
With jealousy

After slaughter and feast of blood,
She cooked with many herbs
And pegged the vines on posts
Of wood to round the fire
She bid they sit upon the vines
To watch her cook
The fire rose, fed by scented wood, and
Boar skin sizzlings, singing the low-flying clouds,
Their senses full with mouthwatering ecstasy
They soon fell one on another to devour
And all approached the raging fire
And blinding smoke in maddened hunger
Soaked by blood

Woman leapt and looping vine and posts
Around the frothing maddened mob, four score,
Trussed them all and tossed them to the fire
And only three escaped, or so I'm told,
To bring despair to other lands, your faithful

And humble, much derided scribe
She cooked them well and brought to end
What started well, and she exclaimed:
What use fertility without bloodlust strength
To protect, defend my own,
From this day I will care with love,
Guile and cleverness, too,
But rise vengeful, blood-enraged
To defend the lives of those I love

The ancient god blinded with tears
From fat-filled smoke, and fallen voracious
Upon the sizzling roasted boar,
To his regret, did not hear her vow,
Not magic ring, or sword, but brute-force love
Would give her strength forevermore

The ancient god saw his creation's grace,
And lust but also hate was born
Toward this pair of creatures he had called
To fill the Earth with living things of his invention
He could not live, but only stand
Aside and watch their lives
They should not be who live this life but he

THE HUMBLE SCRIBE HURRIES THE TALE ALONG

Here, to your relief this time, dear reader,
Your humble scribe intervenes
Our poetical author has not
Yet brought our heroes to meet—
It's not just you I scold—

So let me bring this to an end, or try,
Sad would be to tell, and incredible,
Every tale of man and woman before they met
Water and food they never lacked
But no direction for they left no trail to keep
Their many times coming and going crossed
Never seeing the other until one day
By choosing of the god
And pent-up yearning, burning by his design,
Took a turn around a rock
And fairly fell into each other's arms
The woman screamed and the man gasped
Or so, I, poor, ignorant, intrusive scribe decide,
For at this point the story is not clear
My saddened heart preoccupied with their plight
Did not hear, but gasp and scream there was
And I will ascribe as seemly seems
Someone screamed and the other gasped
And fell into each other's eyes
A sun-filled day and moon they stood,
And once again, before they spoke,
Their voids had filled with love, eternal love
Dear reader, do not respond with mockery
But lose yourself in hope and youth regained,
Your modest scribe who reminds
That youthful love transforms the world
To livable mutability

The ancient one planned well
The world would fill of living things
But little need of adding pain and loss to love
For that is all love is and will ever be
For in the moment of ecstasy, they saw

The day of loss and death for them
And all their progeny and every living thing
Even the rocks below and the sky above
But from this terror dream, they woke
And said, "We live"

That was their marriage vow
Never has there been a better one
They did what lovers do and woman bore
All living things and these soon learned
Their multiplicity, she went on to bear
Many children sprung full-formed
Into the world, to quickly move away
Never heard again, and filled the world
For the ancient god could contemplate betrayal,
Pain and death, every child's ingratitude,
But raising children was beyond the pale
And since he planned to claim her soon as she
Had spread her kind to forever adulate
And sacrifice their goods to him
He did not want to curse himself with raising them
Here your poor wretched scribe must interject,
O, hateful god for humankind, ancient one,
But wise in the ways of children,
All evil one virtue has,
And this I mark for posterity

The great plains filled with game both large and small
And fruit of every kind, grass fed all living things
And rain only in early morn, to not disturb sun's joyous
Pass, nor moon's bright glow nor stars' teeming births,
Kept all green and waving heavenward
They bore their pain and joy in equal measure

To taste, hearing, smell, touch and sight attached
Not one thing unalloyed with joy, pain, content, regret
One falling dove, one bug's travails
The birthing pains of fish and fowl, all felt intense
Until their hearts so full bursting upon their minds
Colored every deed, thought, sight and sound with love

Unknown to the ancient one, he had wrought
Not punishment but love,
Compassion infinite for all that lives
And love for the Creation of the One Supreme
From whose love flows all things
Even the hate and selfishness of the ancient gods
And this poor, wretched, humble and derided,
Suffering scribe must add: the ancient one rules today
But not for long, I do implore the One Supreme

THE ANCIENT ONE CLAIMS WOMAN
The ancient one still firm upon his intended deeds
With reveling pride of his created world
Now filling with humankind and progeny
And all living things of all color and size
Arrived to claim the woman
And put an end to no longer needed man

The ancient god exclaimed:
A race of gods will now be born of my seed
And you and your
Plump child-ling progeny will be
For delightful repast, petit dejeuner,
His evil knew no bounds and was
The first debaser of the

Literary elegance of French to
Epicurean grossness making even
My most iniquitous failings
Seem mere peccancy,
My challenged readers do
Not be ashamed to take out your
Dictionary, it will make you
A better and humbled person

You and your progeny will serve
The race of gods, my seed, until
The end of days
He embraced woman then and made to carry her
To mountain lair of distant climes
Where he could gaze upon his world
And see it bow to him below

But she refused and knocked him
Down upon his rump divine
Dear reader, do not despair, but once again
Poor humble, wretched, suffering
And derided scribe must intervene to say,
Though rump divine, man and woman then
By One Supreme's stealth design,
Had the strength, not common now,
To fell the gods and refuse corruption of
Body or soul

And woman said as he hit the ground,
To no one do I belong, but myself,
And that I freely give to him
That has pledged himself to me
The ancient one with determined speed

Unsheathed his sword *as sword he had*
As do all ancient gods, your etc scribe
And made to strike his rival's head
He wrongly thought that force would grant
What guile could not

And here collapsed his plans by own design
As so prefers the One Supreme
Man's painful long ascent from stone and earth
Had leeched his bones and skin with impervious strength,
Except in love, and mighty sword's blow rent
In two both steel and god's resolve

THE HUMBLE SCRIBE RELATES THE END OF THIS TALE

This long tale's completion falls
To your poor scribe whose humble
List of faults, unworthiness, and sins
Disallows him not the final word:
Though circumstance and sin and ancient gods
Still strive to destroy, deceive and use
Humankind perfused by greed, avarice,
Lust and murderous tendency
Man and woman's bond and love
And One Supreme with loving guile
Will find a way to lead us all
Through love and pain and life
No matter what our bent

Ancient worlds of long demise
When life was new and fed upon
Grace divinely and freshly given,

Still tasting of green grass and
Bright fallen rain, live in me so I may
Praise the created world and
The One Supreme
Free of my blinding sin
And I persist:
Woman of this world
Born of God's purest grace,
Great love and most far-reaching dreams,
The thought of her moved the One Supreme
To create her in shape and form
And placed the four winds upon the Earth,
And the currents of the sea to whisper her beauty
The sight of her to froth the waves
The birds' full sweep of the girdling winds
Seeded the sky and endless plains
With succulent fruit,
The plains were made for her to walk
The mountains for her to climb
The air to form our words in praise of her
Our eyes to gaze upon that which
The One Supreme adores
To seek in sky and earth and praise
All things from the One Supreme
And our mouths to sing full-throated
Of the pinnacle of creation through
Which all things pass to birth

And I remind:
Piteous man, with your strength, determined step
And vision far, your dreams of conquest and betterment,
What small regard you have for your heart's stirrings
And blindness to your companion's devotion

Do not desire, strive not in the steps of men,
And the One Supreme will work through you
Beware the risk, the Earth the anvil
And you the blow, the mighty sun
The fire and breath of your shaping and creation
And the heart of humankind will
Be wrought stronger than iron rock
To know right from wrong in cleaving to
The other forevermore and
To love in flawless form and purity

And so it ends:
Her name Star of the Sea
And his Brave Noble Lord,
The first of his name,
They lived in love
And in pain
A measured time.

BOOK 3

BEGINNING OF THE JOURNEY FROM THE PLACE OF THE ANCIENT ONE TO THE PLACE TO PADDLE

STAR OF THE SEA DREAMS
We seek what we will never see
The ancient enemy seeks our downfall
And even now weaves deception
Hope and self into seeds of discord
To disperse one current to many
That will strive to war, not unity

Though this land has given us
Fruitful repose, it is the familiar abode
Of the ancient god and gives him
Strength each time he falls
But takes from our number
With each misstep

He rises in the dark to steal
Our breath and dreams
And in day hides beneath each
Fallen leaf, to disrupt our destiny,
Our journey, and in aeons yet not dreamt,
Our children and the Land of the Sun

Death, daring and hunger
A torrent of births, the founding
Of many villages and we will arrive
At the place to paddle, a great river,
Which will bring us to
The great waters of the gods
To which all rivers flow

Our children, and we will be in them
As they are now in us, will bring

Us upon the waters on sturdy boats
And I will be on each headland of
Each stepping-stone to the Land of the Sun

And for each day of strife
There will arise Guarionex
Brave Noble Lord, of his own time
And Star of the Sea, Mother of All,
Of her own time, until the last of our days

There will arise Guarionex,
Brave Noble Lord, the last of his name,
And we the people will flow
Into the humanity of the world
The soul of the world, for the final
Struggle with the ancient one

BEGINNING

Guarionex, the first to bear the name,
The father, victor over the ancient one,
And Star of the Sea, mother of all that lives,
Two, in troth to each as one,
Filled the earth with all our clan
Father to daughter and son
Mother to sister and child.
Each deep hollow, mountaintop
Open verdant plains
Afforested primeval lands
Barren sands, each stream's curve
Or depth, found simple *bohio*
Of leaves and wood
And running naked laughing children
Around communal fire

When they thirsted, the sky in darkest mood
Would cloud and weep, and when
They lay to sleep and embraced the earth
The earth would pulse with joy
Give fruit and grass
And buried tuber breasts
Of flesh as of the earth,
You are of me, the earth would say,
Of earth and rock, wind, sky and rain
I give my flesh so you may seek
In error and in truth, a land of peace
Where Guarionex, Brave Noble Lord
The last to bear the name, of distant times
Will bring you to seek the One Supreme

This country was of tropical climes
They walked and slept in simple clothes
Of spun leaves or none at all
They passed unseen, protected
In consonance with land and sky
Moving with the sound of wind-rustled
Leaves, speaking in the chimes
Of a running brook, the calls of birds
Discerning a hidden path lit by the stars
Against the purple black of the veil
That covers the face of the One Supreme
Only by risking each unstable step
That seemed to slide them off
A precipice, but free of shame
And spurning cowardice more
Than death

O, dear reader, what mistaken
Paths you have taken, how fears have

Misled your steps, you shake with fear
In all your steps, your heralds
Announce but catastrophe
Your dreams pull you to despair.
But not the unknown, nor eternity,
Nor exploding universe threaten you
But your children who pick up arms
To destroy what you have built
And your patriarchs, old men
Who can only hate, even that
Which gave them strength,
And weave deceit, words and gold
Into veils that blind the eye and soul

The people built no thing
Which could not be broken to carry
For Guarionex, the first of the name,
Brave Noble Lord, knew that
The ancient enemy was beaten but
Not defeated, and at every step schemed
For their downfall

STAR OF THE SEA
In brightest bloom she walked
As a flower unseen
In a wooded dale touched
Only by sun and rain

She led through darkest
Wooded canopy,
In vanguard's isolation
Not even Guarionex,

The first of the name,
Brave Noble Lord,
Could match her stride
If the ancient one fell
From my blow, on his rump divine,
She would say, and that
At fiercest light of day,
What fear of menace
That crawls by night of
Overhanging trees?

In sure stride, she walked
Over watercourse dry or wet
Up or down precipice or fallen trees
"We go to water's storm
Where we can paddle to the sea
A world of water that leads
To our waiting home,
Sunburnt plains or darkest mountain
Gloom will not impede our path"

She led by the flight of birds
And by the march and size of clouds
Yes, dearest reader, your most
Humble scribe must interject,
Your instruments give you
North, west and destination
How lost you would be to find
Your way by reading
The world's heartbeat
As did the ancient mariners
And those that walked the wild
Breast of the Old Earth

Guarionex, the first of that name,
Brave Noble Lord,
Would provision water and forage food
And fix the camp at night
And break before morning's
Dusky morn

But even at darkening eve
Or dark gray before the dawn
And under darkest canopy
Where even noonday's light
Did not prevail, Star of the Sea
Pushed on, "Each step now
Saves us many tomorrow"

Under darkest canopy where
No light prevailed
Star of the Sea would find
That one aperture where sun
Conspired with rustling leaves
To insert one point of light and
She would cup her hands
And spill the light from right to left
Light transformed to running stream
Would course ahead to illuminate
Their path

With the light of her cupped hands
Star of the Sea would dress her hair
And leap along the lighted path
As might a fire impelled by
The breath of the One Supreme
Dear unbelieving reader, I feel

Your lack of faith, materiality has
Blinded you to possibility,
In the beginning when innocence reigned
Light would change from particles
To waves as need required
And flow as air and clouds, fast or slow,
And as great rivers or small
Or gather as ponds, where
Light-starved creatures
Would drink and swim
And every day was evident things
That miracles today would seem
But not in your day for your very
Birth, thoughts and deeds have
Changed what is or can be

FADING
Life fades as the light of the setting sun
From strength to strength, strong
And yet, in pause, growing dim
Unbidden evening falls and
Steps to night's domain as
The sun is silenced by the moon
Reduced to pale reflection
And so Guarionex, the first of the name,
Father, led with strength and kept
The ancient enemy at bay
Guarionex, rising, as
A mighty mountain rises
Imperceptibly, and then, in all
Majesty, undone day by day
By wind, sun and rain to sand

And Star of the Sea
Capturing the fire of the
One Supreme used it
To lead the way and
Prodded with fiery words
And sight, to climb countless
Mountain ranges and fords
After many climbs and falls
And victories found that others
Were better suited to lead the way

GENERATIONS ARISE
The nights and days
As pearls of darker and lighter hues
Strung on the path they pursued
Preserved memories of joy
And communal love, and also
Of sudden loss, blood and precipitous falls
Each pearl a generation born
As another passed away
Until at evening's fire, they only sang
Of yesterday's trail and morrow's sun
The ancient one whose hand unseen
Plagued their every step forgotten
And Guarionex, Brave Noble Lord,
The first of the name, a dim remembrance
Though his courage, and arm of strength
Still flowed in blood of all the young
And surfaced when the path was lost
By calamity, despair, recalcitrance
Some of nature, self or circumstance
But the worst, a subtle play of fate
By the ancient one

And from these times of journeyed loss
Los Perdidos did arise
For every day they were lost
And only found through
Heart's rage to reach
The land of the sun
And they were named:
Guarionex, Brave Noble Lord,
The driver of humankind,
Guarionex, Brave Noble Lord,
The founder of the tribes of humankind,
Guarionex, Brave Noble Lord,
In the *bohio* he rested,
Guarionex, Brave Noble Lord,
Of the place to paddle,
Guarionex, Brave Noble Lord,
Of where the waters meet the sky,
And others too many to recall
And each and others receded
To memories of deeds not wrought
By men but gods

Their stories all were sung
Of how they impelled the journey
When all despaired and failed
Days without end, now
Almost forgotten, for days
As water-drops shape
Great caverns from solid stone,
Wash away remembrance
Of songs and words of
The most worthy of men
And these in time were lost
To memory as Africa slid

From close embrace
To distant lands

And Star of the Sea,
Mother of all the earth and
Who held the sky in place
Who illumined the path
At start of every day
In darkest canopy and
In blinding sun that seared
The snow of mountains to ice
In marshes sodden with mud and
Slithering worms that entered
At every cavity to have their fill
Here the ancient one would laugh
So resoundingly that few could hold
Their footing on the shaking earth
And many fell headlong to be devoured
Painfully inside in monthlong
Repast by his minion hordes
What part, dear reader, do you play
In your pillowed, heated abode
In his mirthful tortures of your days?

And Star of the Sea,
Mother of all, the pillar of the soul
Of humankind, in shape and form
To presence the One Supreme
Passed the grace of her step and smile
Her athletic, long-boned, cinnamon
Silhouette, and fury in protective love
So when the path grew dim
Or disappeared in the aeons of the trek

Another Star arose, by which the clan
Could discern its way
And from these times, did rise
Las de Caridad
And they were named, in turn,
Star of the Sea, Mother of All,
Light that Beckons,
Star of the Sea, Mother of All,
Embrace of Communal Love,
Star of the Sea, Mother of All,
Fire of the Home,
Star of the Sea, Mother of All,
Voyager in the Place to Paddle,
Star of the Sea, Mother of All,
Caridad of the Deep Waters

Their stories were told and sung
And still are passed at birth
Of each offspring, for each
Sank a pillar into the hearts of
Humankind, which even now
Sustain the roundness of the Earth
In its ceaseless rounds, and
The protective canopy of the sky
And you, dear reader, do you see
Or are you as blind in light as in
Most profound night?

BOOK 4

GUARIONEX, BRAVE NOBLE LORD, FOUNDER OF THE TRIBES OF HUMANKIND

THE WAY
In their long trek though misery
Preyed on their every step
Joy and happiness led the way
For certainty of their own strength
As well the help assured of all in circumstance
O, my dear, uncomprehending
Reader, even now you summon your hope
That they may live through adversity
And find their paradise where
Effort and worry are superfluous
The passive nature-joined joy of
Original humankind unsullied
By modern mischief and greed
Just as you hope for yourself
Don't lose hope, you goad yourself,
But they were no addled fools;
They knew hope the poisoned milk
From the breast of the ancient one
Religion not the opiate of
The masses but hope,
Don't fear despair but hope,
Despair inspires its own vanquishment
But hope, a passive trust of miracles,
And worse the mercy of the powerful
A mystic joining with a primal source
Hope, the parasite that enters
The heart of humankind through
The portal of sloth and naïveté
Hope derides, decays all things

And is slowly buried by the sediment
Of passing inactive days
Adversity brought the named ones
Of Guarionex and Star of the Sea
Strength in wrestling and subduing it
And perception and knowledge
In finding its weakness
Where evil was imbalanced and easily
Tipped into the chasm, and how
Blind greed may be led astray
Guarionex, the last of his name,
And all that came before him,
Welcomed adversity
Each day at peril of death
Made them stronger, no hope of
Skirting danger, achieving paradise,
Eventual victory, prevailing
In circumstance, or in blind or
Sighted luck, but knowing
That each battle, each blow,
Even in each death and in
The demise of all the clan,
Including those not yet born
By foe or Earth's collapse
They would fall in courage
With upraised fist, with support
And love of all the clan
That is the defining intactness
Of hope and faith
One is of the ancient enemy
And the other the clarion
Of the presence,
Even in death and defeat,
Of the One Supreme

THE HUMBLE SCRIBE READS THE CLOUD OF UNKNOWING

"The regular course of causes in creation"
Followed day upon day, one settlement
Upon another, a chain of links,
A flow of blood, thought and faith
From before the beginning, the undesired
And unthought entrance upon this world
From a boundless death, a blind not-self
Not named, darkly shapeless and still,
Without intent
To a path won by
Defeat of uncalled events
Stretching toward destiny
The whispered beckoning
Of the One Supreme

Humankind but silver tendrils
Bubbling, seeping from mountainside
An action of clouds, rain and
Earth, sparking intent
Dreaming force, community, destiny
Under gentle pull of gravity
Drawing slender threads to
Cascading rageful flow to the
Great waters of eternity

THE HUMBLE SCRIBE SPEAKS OF HISTORY

These stories, of aeons so vastly passed,
That humankind was not otherwise
In wakeful stance, were once ascribed
To whom they did pertain

Have now been loosed to all the world
So that the flood survived by
Guarionex, Brave Noble Lord,
Of where the waters meet the sky
Is now ascribed to an abstract king
Of a darkened sea
And the great meditations of
Guarionex, Brave Noble Lord,
In the bohio *he rested, a slender*
Athletic man, imputed to
A rotund, distant, enlightened man
And the founding of a great city
Of world repute wrought by
Guarionex, Brave Noble Lord,
The founder of the tribes,
Is now repeated throughout the world
As wrought by wolves
My dear misled readers, what use
Ancient history, Greek and
Roman myths, when carelessly
Attributed?

THE FIRST SETTLEMENT
On that endless march what lay ahead
Could not be discerned, many directions
For one certain path, many wanderings and false paths
Yet always forward and what lay behind
A spreading tapestry, of small and large families
The batata discovered drew five families to stay
And a pond or lake with fish, three,
Quinoa meant many lost to farming
So those at the head seemed a fertilizing wave

And their fruit were humankind left behind
To thrive in their wake, and loners, hunters,
Potters, solitary holy men and women
And wandering traders took up
Or invented crafts, inspired by
The future promised by the trek,
The present embodied by the families
Which were but one and
The past of the ancestors
That had sacrificed so
The present may exist

As fingers of one hand, one intent,
One heart and mind, anticipating
Thought and action, evoking it
From each, young and old,
And what opportunity was wanting
Called forth for shaping, they
Explored the land and went forward
Taking sparingly what was needed
Giving generously without request

As these small groups evolved to clans
They developed special skills and
Became more themselves, it is here that
Guarionex, the founder of tribes, devised
The idea of founding a city that in concentrating
The resources of the small settlements would
Impel the trek forward to the Land of the Sun
As well as support the survival of those staying behind

LA MESA DE DIOS (AS IT WOULD BE KNOWN IN FUTURE TIMES)

Not long after the creation,
The One Supreme, moved by pity,
In pity knowing that humankind
Overlooked the presence of
Benign eternity and to help in this
There would need to be created
Places on this Earth that in their
Most sublime beauty would signal
That presence to all wandering lost
In a world subject to mortality
Such was La Mesa de Dios
It is mortality that is the root of all evil,
Not money whose evil rises from being the most
Mortal creation of humankind, gold in
Its impermeable counter to flesh
Awakens the lust of flesh

Guarionex was first to see
A densely wooded mountain marked
By rough-spread uplifted rocks,
Brittle iced ponds, and a great open
Fertile valley fed by gentle streams growing to
Rivers flowing from a ring of seven soaring hills
And in the center gently elevated
So as to receive the light of day
From morning to evening sun, and to be smiled upon
By a fulsome moon, protected from strong winds
And lashing rain by the protective hills, truly
A table at which only a God would sit,
La Mesa de Dios, but meant for humankind

By each western hill, entry was protected,
And by each eastern, egress found,
At the center of the mesa a giant rock
Already swept clean and flat by wind and rain
For sitting a city, the center for a meeting
Of past and future, so obviously blessed
That not even the sins of humankind
Could despoil

This city, the central knot of our journey
Tying together the past, all those left behind
To productive labor and increase,
The present to reward their labor
And supporting the future journey

"To tie all our people into a weaving
Of effort and skill from which a great nation
Will rise to rule the ancient lands of birth
The mountains and great plains fed by
Rain and sun and the great waters and
As the Land of the Sun will be our center
Of spirituality, so shall this city be our centered self
And the body of our ancestors",
So Guarionex in one great speech established
That some will fish, others harvest, some explorers be,
And priests will rule at journey's end

The march of many thousands stopped suddenly on
That great mountain overlooking La Mesa de Dios
And as those behind pushed on those ahead
Many tumbled down, laughing and cursing
And these people who knew only the trek
And how to defeat nature in every trick

Of subsistence, now became a people
With a center and a hearth not to be
Broken at each morn and moved,
And they spread to all the surrounding hills
So all could see, even the smallest of the young,
Many of whom in wonder took first step that day,
And anticipate stepping onto the Blessed Mesa

What started in joy, ended in grief,
One, one by one, then all began to toss
Toward the farthest reaches of sky
Songs of loss of all their great
Who had lost their lives so they may live
And recounted every strife
Expelled all grief so their tears made
Their way in misty streams to join
The rushing rivers down below
Lost dreams, ancient loves were exorcised
Ghosts of children, parents, even animals
That accompanied and befriended them
All doubts and hates and conflicts
Were recounted, betrayals also in thousands counted,
And some bowed before the offended or offending ones
And asked forgiveness and forgave
The accumulated evil of great suffering and fear
Exploding in song and dance and regret and loss

After many days of song and dance of grief
A great fear grew, reached out, and
Enveloped the camp, they could not move one step
Toward the Mesa for burdened with all
The remnants of their sins and self-betrayals
They would pollute, destroy its holiness
And bring down the gleeful final punishment

Of the ancient enemy who knew well all their
Revealed and unrevealed sins, many beyond forgiveness

This was followed by a wordless movement
A fiery moment of clarity free of intent and desire
But with an otherworldly strength
That moved them as wind bends the grass
Toward a great precipice that lay directly
On the path to La Mesa de Dios
My love for you, dear reader, warns
That the ancient one can twist
Even repentance, witness of holiness,
And hatred of him to his own ends
Awaken! Brave Noble Lord, and
Mother of All

Guarionex, Brave Noble Lord,
Of the name Guarionex, not handed down
From father and mother to son
Not by birth or sovereign's or cacique's right
But by designation of the One Supreme
Other times by acts that deemed men
Worthy of the name and acclamation of the clan
And by the joining of Star of the Sea,
Mother of All, who in each generation
Would appear, from birth high or low
To stand and lead by the side of Guarionex
And to recognize, acclaim the presence
Of Guarionex of that time who would
Rise as great tasks rose to be done

Guarionex, Brave Noble Lord,
And Star of the Sea, Mother of All,
In contemplation of good and evil,

Hands joined for many days,
Reviewing the byways of future sins,
Now rose and walked to the precipice
In tandem voices, one for the ears of humankind
And one for the souls of humankind,
Touching flesh and spirit exclaimed:
"If this is wise, we both will walk
The precipice paying with our lives
Your past and future sins, and others
Will arise to lead as has always been"

This great group now leaning to the abyss
As flowers of many colors may open
Over many days to greet summer's promise
One petal and then another uncurling
Toward the sun turned toward
Guarionex and Star of the Sea,
Guarionex then exclaimed:
"Turn toward me, I have led you, your sins
Fall under my command, you are born again
And as children enter to this land,
And with my death you will be free,
To continue the trek
But not until this city rises"

The sun had yet a quarter turn to fall
Beneath the Earth, and in silence,
Disturbing neither beast, nor bird, insect
Nor the grass itself, they moved down and up
And slept the first night on
La Mesa de Dios

A VISION OF THE LAND OF THE SUN
The dreams of the Star of the Sea
Saw the Land of the Sun in the midst
Of great waters, an unforgiving turmoil
Of swirling descending liquid caverns and
Towering walls of moving thunder,
Nothing withstanding, where enemies would be lost
But indigenous would thrive, an opal on an emerald sea
Bathed by light of a rising sun, buttressed from wind and
Surf by mighty rising stones as hammered
By the old maker to sit and view the world
And La Mesa had all but the sea and destination to please
For a journey of aeons is a weak stitch to make
In dressing for a future, and a stronghold,
An anchor as this, would ground the future possibility

A stone table of a hundred acres on
A thousand of fertile earth prepared
To diverse abundance of fruiting plants
And trees, wild manioc, batata, quinoa
And many unnamed, a rainbow of flowers
And a mild incline a scampering child
Could descend to bring water
From always flowing rivers
"Here we rest to build and store the many steps
And years still ahead of our journey"

THE FIRST DAY
The sun had not yet turned toward the day
When Guarionex raised the people with
A braying louder than the bulls of the plains
Under the dark night shadow of La Mesa de Dios

He placed two young men with sharpened sticks,
One to run north at sun's first rays, the other west
To mark the expanse of the walls to guard La Mesa
Being young and lithe, they ran too fast at morn
Too slow by evening's fall, just right for a day
Of work, said Guarionex

THE SECOND DAY
Two others were sent the next day to mark
The western and northern walls where the gates
Would be placed, the northern gate to continue the journey
And the western gate to welcome all those left behind
So flow of goods and people would be continued
These would be gates for humankind,
Not holy or unholy but for all
"And those that guard the way will not surrender
La Mesa but with their lives"

THE THIRD DAY
And at the apogee of the sun
When shadows disappear beneath one's steps
All brought the finest of the house
The found, the grown, the stolen, the made
All seeds and fruit and woven goods
All is for all and we begin at birth,
Exclaimed Guarionex,
"You are my children, and none do I put above
Or below, we live for all and build for all
Take as you will, and give what is asked
Plant, build, make, gardens in and out of walls,

Time enough in the Land of the Sun
To grow fat and burdened with goods"

THE WALLS WERE BUILT
A mix of wet claylike earth, stones,
Plants and trees slowly dried
Thick walls, layer by layer, rose
The height of three men
The northern wall shorter
But with an open lattice of stout trees
Matching the height of the other walls, and
To capture the sun for the inner garden
That would supply the people
In case of siege by the many hunters
And wild forest clans that humankind
Had disturbed on their long journey

The inner gardens and other dwellings
Were built, as well the quarters of Guarionex,
On the stone slab smaller mesa
Which was named Guarionex's table
And soon all had huts and gardens
And tools that belonged to them,
And were not jointly shared,
Some lived above, some inside,
Some outside, some near, some far
Others carried water for all, some worked on
A harvest while others rested, perusing
The landscape for enemies, or administering
Goods and services for all, some were thin
Others stout, but all helped all, and none fell
Without many hands to help arise

The buildings of Guarionex's table grew in size
But they were for him and Star of the Sea,
And those that helped,
Though Star of the Sea preferred to rest
At night at her cousin's *bohio*
Even Guarionex's family, brothers and sisters
Lived in the outside village to equally share
The burden of all, his next-oldest brother looked
With judgment and felt he too should live
Within the walls

Slowly Guarionex ruled more than guided
And more of what he ruled belonged to him
And to his dominion,
His rulings became orders not requests,
Gentle urgings became instruction then criticism,
Then interrogation, and finally punishment
As Midas in diseased obsession to turn all
To gold or stone, so did Guarionex
In exaltation see in all he did
The presence of the One Supreme,

Who walks more a king, inspiring others
To courage than a man in grace,
In the work of divinity and eternity?
And who more a tyrant, who sees
Himself as the hand of the One Supreme?
So love turned to fear and fear to hate

STAR OF THE SEA REMEMBERS A DREAM
Star of the Sea, keeper of the fire,
Who yet had not that name
But who as a young maiden

Had made keen notice of Guarionex,
Brave Noble Lord,
The Founder of the Tribes of Men and
Builder of Cities, who also yet had not
The name, had a dream as a stripling girl,
Bathing at a river's shore,
El Escondido of later name,
Which surged from underground
As from the mountain's womb
She was approached by a lioness
Of the hills, carrying a swaddled human cub
In its jaws, as it fell into the hands
Of a frozen Star of the Sea she saw
That its beating heart was outside its chest
She pressed it to her chest to give suck
And then awoke
Dreams of destiny in a child
Are dreams dreamt of future presence,
Of future deeds, of loneliness deferred,
Of a parent redeemed of abandonment, neglect,
Of repair of self, a void where love or relatedness
Should rule, but which remains unstirred
And inhabited by shadows that laugh
And cry beyond our ken and feel

END OF RULE
And as need arose, Guarionex appeared
As did Star of the Sea, but need also calls
The end, a slow decline of day-by-day
Not noticed till final grief, or sudden fall,
As thunder in a sunny day,
Or *huracan's* assault

Harsh rule and punishment
Don't drown rebellion's fire
But compress it to flameless burning of
Resentment that grows in heat
And then explodes, the city thriving
On the rules of an iron hand
But bled by privilege of just a few
Became not a tribe or family
But many heads feeding on opportunity
Losing sight of the trek ahead
Discord and many would-be chiefs
For every one appointed
Ended all enterprise in strife

"Perhaps," Guarionex one day replied to one
Of Star of the Sea's questioning looks,
"I wrongly thought that day by the cliff
That thoughts of past sins threatened
Their resolve, and it was the loss of the
Lion's innocence in hunting the lamb
The innocence of suckling at the Earth's breast
As the fruit is kissed by sun and rain
And abundantly grows assisted without
Judgment by the forest creatures
So did we grow and prosper, thinking not
Of death, nor sin, nor justice, nor mercy
Nor fulfillment, but only the way and
The next day's trek, in tasks we differed
But all was shared, and we slept in each
Other's dreams
Now strife is the day's first meal
And discord the second, possession
The third, we dream of self and
Not the other"

"Perhaps," Star of the Sea interjected
As Guarionex drew a deep breath
For a self-deprecating sigh,
"The city is for some and not for others
Your heart is misplaced and it is for
The lion of the forest and myself to suckle you
The lion cannot live inside walls
Humankind needs walls and cities to fulfill
Its destiny and reveal the meaning
Of the word to be uttered by the One Supreme
And the answer of the ancient one
But others must find the way that traverses
The world, the seen and the not seen,
The days of suns and moons and stars
And the wild rush of this burning torch
That carries us to cold infinity
A mother's love and a warrior's ruthlessness
You are of the way, come, the path
Has been paved by the One Supreme
But only in a divine wisdom, not
By our sight nor understanding"
And so Guarionex surrendered power
And the way of the world, a path that
Turns only on its own desire
Desire, the fountain of sin, and hope
Its incarnation, while love is freely
Given in mortal embrace
In defiance but acceptance of death

THE RESUMPTION OF THE JOURNEY
It was said his brother killed him
Out of jealousy, or traders of goods
In revenge of taxes imposed, and that

The many who left took the body to hide their crime
But others said they had seen Guarionex,
His face shining with peace and self-content,
Pointing to the far horizon exclaiming,
"To the headwaters of the place to paddle
Where starts the watery way to the
Great waters in which rests the Land
Of the Sun"

The city went on with those who stayed
And served its purpose well, the young
Who knew no other way, and the old
Still dreaming the forest way but with
Legs and bones that needed rest

Guarionex with each step slowly shed
The sins of power and authority
Loving more Star of the Sea and her counsel
Even as the steps left to him decreased
Women with child, and the young, even the old
Who preferred forest burial to wall interment
Followed them

Guarionex and Star of the Sea walked
Until one and then a second pair of steps
Followed a small decline and burbling brook
To a flowered copse *and, there, dear reader,*
You may find two sets of bones undisturbed,
Even unto this day, in gentle embrace

BOOK 5

THE PLACE TO PADDLE AND THE GREAT WATERS

THE PLACE TO PADDLE
These were people of the great forest
And children of its every clime
Barefoot and unclothed, shod and clothed
When need called, the leaves, the very rocks
And wind rose up, the creatures of the sky and the
Scurrying ones of the canopy, and those that lived
In holes of wet earth, even those, the unseen
And shadowed ones beneath the leaves of the forest floor
Working as the hands and breath, the very will
Of the One Supreme

All these taught them well of how to build,
Maintain and live in this world
Even the sun and rain, the moon,
The calls of night-moving creatures,
All that lived and all that perished to feed
The lives of the great forest, and provide
The pillars, the warp and woof of history,
Continuity, of the great forest, never sleeping,
With a dark-green mane as a horse of war
And the soft yielding breast of the first mother

These were people of the great forest
And became as all the creatures
And knew every one, its ways, thoughts
Its love of offspring, its love and joy
Of every dawn, or eve's approach
They saw the birds' shape and how
They sailed the wind, and wondered if
With such wings they could sail the
Great waters to come, and the spider's

Spinning as home, net and silk,
And the bee's industry, frugality,
Community and fertilizing skill
The earth, the rain, the ant, the sun
All had their lessons, secrets, skills

And as the seasons flow as the sun
Recedes or nears, and their journey took
Them over bare-rocked snowy mountains,
Verdant lowlands, and troubled rushing waters
They learned the place of the great forest
And their own, within a greater scheme
Not open to understanding, but to discovery

And so upon an extraordinary day
In aeons extraordinary, Dawn signaled
The Sun's approach, her face
Turned toward the coming day
Both arms, as clouds clothed
In flowing linen of orange, yellow, pink dye
Carelessly spilled from above,
Pointed toward the lightening gray edge
Where earth meets sky, her billowing hair
Flowing onto her womanly back
Made Night pause his retreat
To fully embrace his eternal nemesis
Always out of reach at peril of his dissolution,
But Evening stayed his hand, I give myself
To you at every end of day, we need preserve
Balance of night and day and you
Will come with me

Dawn, who in previous lives, had loved
The kindness of Star of the Sea

And never dimmed her heavenly light
Painted the place to paddle in bright red
And directed the Sun's rays so
The river shone as a ruby bracelet
For all to see

The hillside encampment, waking
From arduous days of travel
With one voice exclaimed
Orinoco, and so it was named

THE LAUNCHING
And there the multitude launched itself,
As the thundering waves of snow
Snap and capsize trees in unstoppable descent
Or as rivers and lakes in flood's disgorgement
Overrun their boundaries and fill the valleys
And carve new pathways of silver lacing
Or as flocking birds at evening time
Overwhelm the sky with pirouettes
For movement's sake and land as one,
And left behind all the goods and crafts
That could not be used in water life
Or to assemble rafts and carve canoes

They worked at day by sun and
At night by torch and moon and stars
Until a flotsam chain of flesh, cloth,
Wood and craft, as the wreckage of
A great ship named Land's Journey,
Preceded by cheers and shouts
And leaping fish, and even curious
Denizens of the dark forest on both sides

Northward flowed toward
The arc of the sun, the Land of the Sun
They marveled as they seemed to fly
On the swift water as the birds fly
In the wind, some prayed for wings
And dreamt and told stories of winged gods
And men, others noted that craft with goods
Piled high caught and were impelled by the wind
But most just sat and gave feet,
Legs and back a rest and swore by
All the gods, even some made up
And given names on the instant
As ruling the river or sky and birds,
They would never return to land

TRIP TO THE GREAT WATERS
At every shallow or waterfall they
Disembarked and after provisioning
From the forest's bounty
Would have a great feast that lasted weeks
Stragglers could catch up, and merchants of goods
From the great city would come to trade
And messengers, or those dispirited,
Requesting help or goods would be sent back

If the surrounding land was bountiful in fertile
Forest gods, some of the young and old would stay,
Such a life was a healthy one and produced
Strong fertile women and men, and in the
Centuries since the first raft to the swifter
Canoes, many children were born and grew
And the people were strewn as one might
Spread flower petals along the banks

Of a river that wound through half the world
In celebration of a happy marriage of water and land
They walked on land as creatures of the forest
And farmed it as the creatures that lived in the earth
And understood as birds who see the vast
Geography of land, mountain, desert, valley,
Sky and water, how the heavens and what
Comes from underneath, all, live in harmony
And dependency, one on one and one on all,
And how all is one, and how man and woman
Also are part of this, even this small clan,
Now growing large, fleeing the ancient enemy
An impossible task, my dear reader, and here
You have my heartfelt sympathy for your
Eternal vulnerability, because the ancient one
May disguise himself as a small stone that
Is carried as keepsake, or any item in
A hiker's knapsack, or being essential spirit
One may give him portage disguised
As an idea of essential merit,
Does not humankind kill wantonly
Even in the name of the One Supreme?
Are we not all blasphemers, assiduously
Engaged in the ancient one's designs?
But Guarionex and Star of the Sea's offspring
Were much lesser sinners for they knew
Of the ancient one's immanence and based their lives
On the body of the forest and the river
And had only sticks and stones
As engines of destruction, how unlucky
You are

THE FIERCE PEOPLE OF THE FOREST
There were other people of the forest and rivers
But one more noble than the rest and
Surpassing fierce
Though living in peace among themselves,
They had learned hunter is safer than prey
Their precedency, so was it said,
Was a great city of beginning times,
Blessed by fertile lands and flowing rivers,
Sweetened by endless groves of
Flowering grasses and trees.
Creatures of the sky, earth and water,
And of the mountains and the plains
Would come to drink and would grow fat,
Indolent, easily harvested prey,
The water stored in skins, replete with sugar
And mixture of fruit and seeds by the hand
Of wind and nature's chance, would ferment
To a sweet wine that ornamented every meal
Of every day, the five meals of day extended
To the borders of each so there was only one
That began at sun's rise and ended at
Sun's return,

Finally, no need to rise at dawn, but for
Refilling of the skins, for the animals, lions
And crocodiles, and other husky beasts
Were trained (here, my dear, credulous reader,
I will rely on your trust, well earned, in me
Though farfetched as this might sound,
I have observed much evidence in support
Of this in private archeological collections)
To prey on the smaller but succulent beasts

And deliver them to the masters' doors, or
Entryways, for a drink of intoxicating elixir
Needless to say, their opulent blessings
Could not defend them against any of
The nomadic raiding groups, and soon
The city fell and disappeared from recall
Whatever small band survived, stripped
Themselves of fat and goods and swore
To survive by wits and strength
It is supposed that this fierce band
Impelled Guarionex and Star of the Sea's
More peaceful clan to flee before their spread
But both peoples knew not to encroach
On each other's journey, and except for
Some disputes proceeded to their destiny

LAND, WATER, SKY
A trinity of reality, the hard substance
Of every day, but one or even two
Does not suffice as stage for human life
Add Sun's embrace, the fuel and nourishment
Which calls forth the flesh, and Wind's
Whispering, in the flight of birds,
Of an eternal soul, a mix of breathing wonder
That turns our eyes and thoughts to eternity

A WATER LIFE
Barefoot along the edge, perilous crossings
Of still and raging waters, sudden clefts
Ending peaceful paths in chasms and cragged
Cliffs of sheer rock, descending with each

Handhold a risk to progeny yet only dreamt
And ascents where many fell to be swept away

Water seeps from mountain breasts in languid
Pools, shallow ribbons gathering weight
From birth to awkward flow in step or two
To husky adolescence and then broad-shouldered
Strength, biting deeply earth and stone,
Still ministering to creatures of Earth and sky
But now teeming with creatures of its own devise
Eels, caiman, piranha, many finned, unfinned
And legged, crawling, shapeless and shelled
Swimming, floating, rooted denizens

A deeper watercourse, a place to paddle,
Supports rafts, simply lashed, from there
Canoes of bark or skins, and observed buoyancy
Of trees felled by wind or age, an idea born
Trees burned out and shaped, conceived by
Children with firewood or old men excused
From the hunt and carving wood as toys,
Ancestors or effigies of gods,
And sails from the effects of wind or flight of birds

To catch a monkey in a land of trees
Is best impelled by amorous simian
Intentions than flat-footed hunger of
An ape long ago fallen from
The canopy, but to catch a fish that swims
In hordes from the eagle's vantage-view
Of floating raft with sharp taloned
Blows from bows and practiced hands
One may thrive, a family too,
And generations of progeny

ORINOCO CITY

A city or a people are not measured in height
Nor cohesion, nor unity of purpose
Nor blood, but as a living organism
Each part, each limb and process receiving and
Giving life without tribute or tariff
And so a great city, a city of waterways,
Some broad with fast swelling currents, and others
Of still pools brimming with penned aquatic life
Hemmed in by islands, spots of land, one upon
The other easing into broad fertile plains
Of grasses and tuberous plants slowly rising to forested
Expanses of brilliant green shading into
Dark-green nights where the sun could not be seen
And mountains, on distant view, their ancient age
Capped by white manes and shawls

Words shouted from shore to shore or whispered
And carried on the fire's flames of evening's meal
Quickly coursed through the limbs and senses
Impelled by the city's heart seeking relationship
And body's unity, so all things, good or bad,
Must exist in all parts, shared, recognized
As the story that will be passed on to progeny
Dear reader, once again, your derided scribe
Must in all humility interject, do you not see
In your great nation, that breadth of words
Does not scale the mountain ranges nor
Outlast the journey of endless plains, nor
Encompass the simple unity of this water world
Though your science impelled the thunder of the sky
And the bristling ether that surrounds
To carry words and tragedies of every day
To even the edges of the universe

So all things, all inventions, signs of hands
Grunts, howls, words, smoke, paper, writing,
Cities, philosophies, armies, war, love,
All invented to communicate, enforce
Your purpose, destiny, relatedness including
Your fearsome destructiveness?

TO THE GREAT WATER STEPPING
Guarionex, Brave Noble Lord, the caller
Of birds and the son of the wind,
Born and raised on a spit of land
Whose name changed with the vagaries
Of tide from Moon's Arc to Bird's Tongue
As the former a slender needle of wet sand
More pools of water with captive fish than sand
And as the latter footing enough for a fishing raft
With sidings and roof of plaited palm leaves
Home for father, mother and son

As a boy he walked in modesty as a small bird might walk
And swam from the raft, in mooring or in the river,
He swam with small and large of the river's
Inhabitants before he walked, it is said,
Even with piranhas, and all those of his name to be
Would be forevermore of land, water and sky
His child-names fit his modesty, Little Bird,
Given him by his father, and Little Tooth,
Given by his mother
When the birds came to feed on the small fish caught
In tidal pools, Little Bird would sit still
Until the birds no longer saw that he was there
And would clamber on his shoulders and head

For better perspective, he learned all their sounds
And every move, so he ran like them and walked
And pecked on fish as a bird but would not eat of them,
And again, your humble scribe must interject to add,
It is said that as a tiny boy he would sit,
Yet not given to discourse with mother, father or clan
Pointing to the sky, the earth and water
Sermonizing the birds that to peck and play
With fish is just, but to eat, to kill is wrong
Large birds and small, black, white
And the speckled birds, the long-legged
Flaming-orange birds, the many-colored
Toucan birds, and their cousins, toucanets
Those that eat and those that don't eat fish
Brought in to argue with stubborn Little Bird,
Little brother of the birds, and fish,
Flying and hopping, trilling in long lines of notes
Even squeals, wings flapping, hovering over him
Flying on long frustrated arcs to clouds and back
No! we have eaten fish, they sang, big, small
Living, dead, since before your tribe
Was ever born,

The birds prevented from eating them
By Little Bird's recalcitrance,
The fish multiplied to such encumbering numbers
That a slow pestilence reached onto the waters,
But still Little Bird stood firm, until finally
The birds called on Old Eagle who was feared
By many of them, they sent the smallest
Of their kind, small and yet not fearing
The great eagle, not even in combat,
Arriving at a craggy mountain top which took

Days to reach with the use of his small wings
He said, Great Old Eagle, I am your servant
In all, except dominion of my own self,
We need you in contest with a boy man
Who would convince that eating fish is sin
The eagle replied in the soothing notes
He used on his approach with food
When nest was full with a hungry brood
Of chicks, (to you, dear reader, it would sound
As the proudful cry of the ruler of the sky)
My small but brave and worthy opponent
Your dominion of your self is as of
My own, of concern to no one else,
Let us go in harmony to this boy man
Who even now fulfills the patterns of the stars
That many years ago announced the birth
Of he who would carve a road on the
Great Waters for the people of Orinoco
To reach the Land of the Sun

On his approach the Great Eagle saw
Little Bird, also called Little Tooth, wave
His arms as though he would fly with them but
Was not able to leave the ground and
Went tumbling back, in his sorties
Even jumping from his humble home's roof
In vain attempt to catch the wind,
But even this would not lift him
Beyond his strong legs' spring
And he tumbled down saying
"Someday, I will fly, when I reach those
Mountains I will jump and fly"
"Keep him on the water until he has a

Man's sense," his mother often warned his father
"Even tied to this boulder," his father would say,
Pointing to a craggy sandstone outcropping
Eaten by wind, water and time to a home
For black-shelled snails, a tasty repast
When boiled in the brackish water of the river,
"He would make the climb and jump"

"Little Bird and Little Tooth, I give you
Another name, Little Cloud, for someday
When you are a Brave Noble Lord, you will sail
The Great Waters as the clouds sail the sky
On the wind," said the eagle who now had shed,
Except in glint of eye, his regal ways
"But you will gather more names, for all the world
Will hear of you, so many names
They will weigh you down to this Earth
But you will have the earth and the waters to play
And the wind will obey your commands
Leave the sky to me and I will be your eyes"
This was said in the call of eagle to its brood,
And to its mate, and even of combat, and also
In the call of ecstasy of dominion when
The stretched-winged eagle, lifted to great heights
By the north wind, crosses the path of the sun
And sees all below is the hand of creation

And Little Bird, Little Tooth, Little Cloud
And yet to be Brave Noble Lord, prancing
In a child's way as man of power, and singing
Fearlessly in the songs of all the birds
That they must not eat his friends, the fish,
This from a son of man and clan whose world

Is built on fish, suddenly saw the world
From a great height, even above the eagle's
Flight, that each part supported the other
And gave as much as took, except for humankind
The Great Eagle sensing this then said,
"Guarionex, Brave Noble Lord, of the Great Waters,
You are now named, launch your people
To the Land of the Sun, and take this bravest
Of messengers, the Pitirre, who fears not
The Great Eagle and will be friend, heart and bond
To us, send him when you need to see the world
From the sky"
Left unsaid, dear reader, that the Pitirre, a small bird
That in combat may defeat even the Great Eagle,
Is native to the Land of the Sun, and now forevermore
Will fly to Guarionex's need

GUARIONEX, OF THE GREAT WATERS, GROWS UP

Guarionex now gave up the childhood things
And wondered how clouds and birds capture
The wind to fly above the Great Waters,
"Little Bird," his father said,
For he knew not his son was Guarionex
And destined to take the voyage no one
Had dared and lived, "First,
You must master the things of men, then
Take a wife and bring children to the clan
And these will teach the working of the world"

Guarionex, the child cacique, by benediction
Of the Great Eagle, ruled rudely

Over his small domain by push
And shove and command, until he found
That kindness and example had best results,
This changed his eyes to see that birds don't work
Their outstretched wings to fly, but fly,
Descend, ascend against or with the wind
By their stance and presence to the wind
It was then, on land, that Guarionex first took
The kingly stance that would win
The clan to him *and I must say*
My love for him

And as he grew, his estimation of self
Fueled in part by clan's laudatory acclaim
And by every endeavor's success,
Fish husbandry yielding enough to feed
Many villages, his skill with a bow
Letting fly his arrows from the highest tree
And like a taloned eagle striking two
Or three of the fattest fish, pulled out
Like precious stones on a necklace,
Thanking the fish for their sacrifice for him
And praying for the welfare of their progeny,
His skill at every sport, and the admiration
Of all the young women his age
Filled him so that he seemed to walk
Lightly on the earth, a bounce, a glide
An easy step, fortune his father and
Luck his mother

Guarionex worked all day and slept all night
As the young sleep, deep, dark and beautiful
In dreams that make you strong in day

Until one day a young woman bathing naked
In the river, as all the young and old always did,
Caught his eye, her ebony skin reflected the sun,
As the great waters at the edge where sky
Meets sea shine a cloudy brightness, which
Refracted her color to yellow and red as quinoa
Singed in a pot, and as she raised her arms,
He thought a flower blooming and
"I, a monarch in search of milk and nectar,
To create a garden of her seed"
But she only laughed when he approached and
Dove into the river's flow and disappeared
That night in troubled sleep, Guarionex of the
Great Waters, searched the river and crouching
Down to see beneath saw a giant bloated toad
And with a start stood up in his darkened *bohio*
Hopped out croaking in four-legged leaps
And dove right in to awake in the cold current
In a night illumined by a moon
That whispered of love with candied breath
He saw a startled long-legged flaming bird
In silhouette run upon the water with flapping
Wings and slowly climb the steps of the wind
Into the sky, a lone bird crossing the face of the moon
"It is the wind that lifts the bird upon its back
And lets it float as on a great unseen river"

Guarionex, Brave Noble Lord, of the Great Waters
Understood two things, that it is the wind that has
Lifted the birds and the birds have changed to leave
The earth and sail the wind, the great land birds
Too broad of width and short of wings through prideful

Refusal to change will never fly, and the second thing
That the wind and water are part of one hand,
The palm and back of hand, which move all things,
Both wind and water are flowing things
And one may swim in both, oars are the wings
For the river, and cloth the wings for wind
It was actually three things Guarionex understood
But the poet engrossed in literary concepts leaves for
Me, your humble scribe, to clarify, and bring us
Into the next scene, he understood he had become the toad,
Ugly and bloated with self-regard, his success not due
So much to him but to the world, the clan and others
Who lifted him up, and it was this that transformed
His heart to beat for him but others too, the world
And all living things, he saw that love keeps all
In consonance, and with startling clarity that
The young woman loved him as he loved her,
She lived at a morning's walk and by Noon
He reached her bohio, both being of age
He extended his hand, and she, noticing his change,
Put hers in his, in unison they said, "We live"
And it was done, her name Star of the Sea, Mother
Of the Way to the Land of the Sun
She said that night to Guarionex, in recumbency,
Where first they met at river's edge, "Put away your bow,
The path we take in this world is not of the world
But save this arrow for me"

Not one moon passed to prepare a sailing vessel
Of bark and wood, a marvel to the clan but of
Easy design, another moon waiting for calmer seas and
The steady west wind, Star of the Sea devised

A way to sail north on east or west wind, for though
Guarionex was brother to all that swims
And walks and flies, and would converse with them
In Arawak or their own calls and notes
Star of the Sea could hear the secret whispers
Of clouds, wind, water and sky, and even fire,
And know their ways that day and plans for the
Morrow, the wind did not know she heard
His fakery to blow this way one day and suddenly
Change the next, and the Great Eagle saw half the world
And told them of coming storms and swells, the Pitirre
Riding comfortably on Star of the Sea's shoulder
Growing fat with special seeds she brought for him
Would do her bidding to search craggy rocks of land,
Volcanic islands, for fertile earth where the clan
Would thrive, she pointed north, "It is Leviathan
We search, for there at the Land of the Sun,
The cows fat with calf go to birth and
By their breach and spout we know
We have arrived at fertile earth"

A ROCKY CLIMB NORTH UPON THE SEA
North they sailed upon the world's back
At first rock fall, a jagged cleaved opal,
Luminescent-green streaked with limestone rock
Nestled in an emerald sea, the Great Eagle
Turned back to his domain, "Pitirre now is your eyes,
A necklace of opal pearls and stone will mark your path
To the Land of the Sun and three large isles of
Fertile earth where your children will know
Happiness, but beware the mountains which
Scorch the earth and the three white birds
From distant lands"

Faithfully, Pitirre would overfly
Each crop of rock they passed
But found each one of mostly barren rock,
Too small for overflow of the Orinoco clan.
They learned how one might sail, though slowly,
Against tide and wind, and how to temper
Favoring winds, they passed many small isles
And one that was but a smoking mountain
Belching fire at night but with an ample lap
So full of fruit trees and small game that they
Stopped one day for restful feast
Pitirre, wary of the smoke and fire,
Sang a defiant song that said, "My eyes
Will not leave this boat as they can see from here
That is a worthless rock," neither Guarionex nor
Star of the Sea pressured him

THE HUMBLE SCRIBE SUMMARIZES

And here we must leave the detailed recall
Of Guarionex, Brave Noble Lord, the last of his name
For here, as I carved his words into clay,
He broke into tears for Guarionex, Brave Noble Lord,
Of the Great Waters, and Star of the Sea, mother of the way
Were his parents to be, as I have heard from other sources,
They found the three larger and fertile islands
That were to be the center for millennia, four
Some say ten thousand years, of a thriving
Culture of land and water, and they returned directly
To lead the clan to the Land of the Sun…
But what is not known, and dear reader,
I hereby swear you to secrecy, is that
On this trip of discovery, these details told in intimate,
Almost embarrassing clarity to me by Pitirre

*With such trilling of notes and shaking of wings
That he was hoarse for days, Pitirre sang in strident notes
That as they sailed toward the Land of the Sun
He noticed the breach and spout of Leviathan
In ritual of fertility, and he flew to announce to the
Behemoth the consummation of ancient legend:
Guarionex and Star of the Sea's arrival
Leviathan, aware of humankind's aspirations,
And in spite of his better judgment, admiring
This small ape's intrepidity, and respectful
Of their distant kinship, upon hearing this,
Lifted their craft on his back
And with much acclamation of celebratory nature
Brought them safely to shore where watching
The festival of birth and impregnation for future years,
Of these great beasts, no strangers
To courtship dances and dalliance,
Guarionex and Star of the Sea
Were inspired to love each other with such
Intensity of love that Star of the Sea
Immediately conceived, and that conception was
Guarionex, Brave Noble Lord, the last of his name,
And Great Eagle, nor Pitirre, nor Leviathan
Nor Guarionex and Star of the Sea, not even in
Her dreams of prophecy and understanding which
Foresaw so much, could foretell that leading
Their people in the first foray of many sailing craft
To the Land of the Sun, their small child,
Not yet named Guarionex, Brave Noble Lord,
For such namings were only rarely passed
Down from father or mother to child
And were and are a blessing, curse and destiny,
Free of lineage, (dear readers, you deceive yourselves*

To think yourselves masters of your own destiny,
For destiny does not know achievement in this world
And true or great destiny is more a curse of suffering
Than of joy and adulation of others, your achievement
Will be your "success," but your destiny will be
A ruined planet, Wake! to reality) never thought
That in the first foray of their many sailing craft
Their child would be snatched from their arms
By a storm and forevermore lost to sea

Though their child was lost, they went on in grief and settled
The middle island, some settled Quisqueya, and others the one
Of the arc, but Guarionex and Star of the Sea settled
The Land of the Sun, on the northwest corner of the smallest,
To be called Borinquen, and also Northeast Quisqueya
And waited through many years of the fertility rituals
Of Leviathan for their child to return, living or dead,
But though they lived long, he never appeared
There by the great cliffs of lime and sandstone and ancient lava flows,
They set a bohio made of plaited palm leaves and wood branches
To come to rest and watch by the restless ocean,
The constant seething waves and wind carved
In sandstone and coral fossil reefs, gargoyle figures
Of awesome aspect, sentinels, crocodiles,
Winged leviathans, Byzantine queen in dress and crown
And opened a hole into the cliff face so deep, some say,
That the waves reached to the center of the Earth and
Quenched the great volcano that once had covered
This land in black stone

As they aged, their grief undiminished grew also for each other,
For they saw each other approaching death
And not of worry for themselves but in grief for the other's demise

They died, the one holding the other and refusing each to go alone
And as one heart flew out from their breath, the other followed
In loving harmony much as they had conceived Guarionex

But now to that eternal change that we call death
Wrapped in palm leaves and the sailing cloth of their old craft
They were given, as requested, to the deep carved hole, El Hoyo,
And the center of the Earth, and it is said by those that have sometimes
Slipped into that maelstrom and managed to swim out alive
The whispers of their love, one for the other, have aroused desire to
Let the current take them to the center of the Earth and not return
And more than one fisherman has spoken of hearing the beating
Of two hearts in tandem, the beat of all that lives
Upon this land and will continue as long as the memory
Of Guarionex and his heart mate, Star of the Sea, survives

And came to pass what they could not conceive:
Millennia passed and their child's name, but now Guarionex,
Brave Noble Lord, was recalled by the One Supreme,
And he was delivered upon this shore, a manatee some say
Or a woman in flowing robes, one night of brilliant stars,
She left him upon the sand and returned to the sea,
And Yumac recognized and gave his name
Guarionex, Brave Noble Lord, but not yet known
As Last of His Name

BOOK 6

GUARIONEX, BRAVE NOBLE LORD, THE LAST OF HIS NAME, IN THE LAND OF THE SUN

LAND OF THE SUN
Sentinels, crocodiles, winged leviathans,
Byzantine queen in dress and crown
Seated and mounted kings, leaping bears
Mesa paths, cut from stone, as hanging ledges
Honeycombed from below,
Moonscape rocks, pockmarked,
Fluted edges sharpened to razor's edge
Fossil chambered nautilus, coral stone
Of all design and shape, water-brushed to reveal
The ancient ocean shells
Peeled back to inner workings,
Water-rammed, deep, pitted caves
That open to Earth's core,
All this, the island too, teetering to be expelled
On continent's falling edge
That shouldered Africa long ago
To drift to Asia's side

GUARIONEX'S SONG OF DESTINY
Spores, seeds and feathered wings are brought upon
These winds and tides to the home of
Guarionex, Brave Noble Lord, the last of his name,
Born a man, and now to die a god
Not divinely sent, but by deeds, and time acclaimed
Not hopeful tales I have to tell
But of long declines and ends

My ancient home of rounded wooded hills
And jutting cliffs with mantled laps of stone
Embracing and rocking the sea

In time to the moon's pulsing tides,
Sea and rock shaping each,
Half-moon coves hewn as by godlike hands,
Boulders strewn as die to read the One Supreme's
Next act, and the long arc
Of the fiery sun to nothingness,
Now illuminating, frenzied, teeming life
Scuttling crabs, birds and fish, mute shelled forms,
Waving coral and seaweed plants
Rolling algae carpets rooted on ancient ocean beds
Lava flows and fossil coral reefs, folded and fluted,
Thrust upward as these same cliffs
The surf pounding and shaping them to gargoyle shapes

This deep Earth, my home, with masses of living things
As the great mane of a sleeping god
Her head the Earth, the moon and Mars a sleep-tossed arm
Her knees the Sun, and feet Jupiter and Saturn
This deep sweet-jellied earth over
Ancient seabed stone
Silted coral spores and shells, compressed to
Mantled lime, overstreaked with black lava flows
And deeper still sanded beaches over coral beds
The most ancient times before the word
Of the One Supreme gave rise to humankind
And its downfall
All creatures know pain and humankind the fall

We walk on this ancient land
Still in throes of
Its flaming birth and
One Supreme's first intent,

Though this song sings
The end of my Earthly stay,
And I, ready to
Prepare the Sun's destiny
On the day that the One Supreme demands
This land is young and yet
To birth the men and gods
That will bring forgiveness's might,
The act of creation and the word that
The Divine intent to speak has wrought,
The expanding light and mass of this
Exploding universe, and Whose Drawn Breath
For first syllable will thunder shake
All things to purity

THE MANATEE

There was no one to see, except the stars,
In the flat coal-black sky,
Mirrored in roiling sea as winking pearls of light,
The dark behemoth's slide around the water-troubled rock
The scuttling crabs all stopped to watch,
White-shadowed forms that fed on them,
Paused one foot upraised, head sideways cocked
Not one crab died that night, nor one
Night-feeding bird by choking happenstance
As water, she leapt upon the sand, rolled back
And on the shore, she left a child of woman born,
His name was mine, Guarionex

Yumac, yet not declared a god,
Killer of trees, who scorched their hearts

With sky-born fire and gave them life again
As ships upon the sea that carried six men,
And another six in weight of fruits,
Fowl and roots to trade along the coast
Lured by silent night, the lack of ocean's roar,
Found me and woke the clan, still asleep
As though in trance induced by vine and seed,
And said, "I set the clan upon the sea
By joining fire, sea, sky and Earth
And now a woman of the sea brought me
This son, Guarionex by name
It was foretold, great sea-born men
Would come to lead, and this my son is he
Who will contest my will?"

No one replied and I was raised by all
But learned to swim before I walked
And rarely left the moving edge where
Sand and sea are mixed
Each tide left the rocks covered with
Lobsters, snails, urchins of the sea and crabs
Descending flocks of birds, and I,
In swooping, laughing leaps
Came down to feed, I swam
The shore and deep, and learned
Every hole and rock called home
By fish or crab, and swam along
With calving leviathan
And sucked also on their great teats

I, Guarionex, explored on land and knew where
All things grew, what lived and died,
What would give fruit, and plants that multiplied

And the living loop of clan, land, sea and sky
That gave all things life, meaning, and destiny,
I stitched with urchins' spines,
And plaited palm frond strings
The sea's salty spray upon my lips
The yielding sand as I ran,
The cooling shade of a thick-leaved tree
A juice-dripping fruit, in Yumac's hands,
Offered to me after a parching noonday Sun
Strung them together all at once
On all four limbs, as banners and kites
Of the days' loving memories, a running child
With colored streamers and whirling leaves
Reaching from the shining shore
Above the cliffs to the dark
Shadowed mountains, each day
Adding more, so the wind would lift
My heart and body too
Above the rough-hewn and sharpened
Rocks that took their daily toll in blood

Upon maturity, strong, dark, long-limbed,
Sharp of eye and mind, and fleet on land and sea,
With beauty graced, in all modesty,
The elders spoke to me the story of our clan,
And in reply, I named each blade of grass,
From village bower to the sea,
For an ancestor and all their progeny,
And each tree by a year in our long history
Each branch a month and leaf a key event
That brought joy or grief to those that lived
In the river of our flesh, from the first man,
Of rock and stone, who came to surface light,

Now encased in these cliffs and rocky shore
And behemoth from the sea, shaped by an ancient god
To most gracious sight, the woman who gave birth
To all living things that we consume,
And now flies so high, a star above the sea,
To observe us below

I named all things with our history, so it
Became a living truth for all to see and know
And this was when it was first said
That he like Yumac was of the gods
I tended these and taught each clan
Within a clan, each man and woman,
Each child, how best to nourish each blade and leaf
So that we had a hundred words for light, rain and green
And as our ancestors' remembrance grew and flourished
So did all living things throughout our range
And even our number grew to watch each blade
Of grass and leaf to help in nourishment
One word in manifold multiplicity
With so many ways to speak it
Grew to name and distinguish each star,
Its path and seasons' moods,
Each blade of grass and leaf, and still have left
Enough at night, by firelight, to name and speak
Of creation's acts and history
And flow to end of time
And this word's color, each hue, meant love

VOYAGES
As our numbers grew and fruit and goods
Increased we traded far from our cove
And befriended the sea and tides

Of our small world, which seemed so vast
Could unrelenting joy and loving work
Create a void of loneliness, fate or age
Much like the sea grinds caves into walls of stone?

Yearning to explore further from our shore
I made west one day, six moons at sea
Along the coast, as many days
As flowers on the red lilac tree,
Emerging from the east to my ancient home
And soon again, cutting the last bedraggled torn
Childhood banner of memories, watching it
Sail to the highest mountain drawn by
A vertiginous wind into dark flickering clouds
I prepared to set upon the sea
To where it meets the sky
To find the Tree of Life to build
A great city in the Land of the Sun

GUARIONEX, BRAVE NOBLE LORD AND THE TREE OF LIFE

A tree to bring together the nations
As one family to live in peace
What better tree for the ships of trade
To join the earth and great waters of this
World with that of heaven and
The daily toil of humankind
To cure the strife that threatens
Our great journey

A great city will rise here to link
To serve as
Conduit if they wish to join

Those that forge ahead, a mighty link
Of a future nation that will serve as the limbs
Of peoples of the Land of the Sun
An errand for a fool and his companion
You say, dear reader, and once I may agree,
Though the tale of the Tree of Life
Was first told to me by Guarionex,
Brave Noble Lord, the last of his name,
I could not believe it true
Or that he would venture and take myself as
Company, no Enkidu I, in spirit nor strength,
(though I did teach Enkidu much
As part of Gil's retinue)

I will spare you the harrowing trip,
After leaving our canoe, over mountains
And dark forests full of beasts, deceitful sprites
And devils, roaring rivers and perilous crossings,
Finally, after many months we arrived
At a great water from which could be seen
An island with a ring of mountains, and an open cove
From which much activity could be perceived
Smoke, sand and distant yells could be seen and heard
We made our way with quickly assembled raft
Praying to all the gods and the One Supreme
That tide nor wave detain or capsize us
As we closed, we perceived a great battle
Between three armies raging, one of black,
Another of yellow and one of white men
Many bodies strewn upon the sand
At Noon's high point they sat, taking rest
From bloody slaughter and chatting among
Themselves and across enemy lines in
Friendly terms as in family gathering in day of feast

GUARIONEX, THE LAST OF HIS NAME, CALLS OUT HIS NAME

I am Guarionex, son of the great one
Guarionex, the first of his name, and
Of all that followed in the call of the name
And of Star of the Sea and all of her name
And son of Yumac, the god who joined
Earth, fire and sea to help us voyage upon the
Waters, it is his craft that brought me here
He is all and father to me, for he found me
Upon the shore of the Land of the Sun
When brought by the goddess of the sea, Caridad,
Who in kindness and greatness delivered me
From the ocean's wrath and the jealous god who rules below
She is all and mother to me and guide
For she taught me the Earth spins
On an uncertain path and is brought
To existence and its own self by acts of humankind
Whose freedom is conceived and granted
By the One Supreme
Caridad taught me the song of the world
And that each creature sings one part
Each melody discordant but together to the hearing
Of the One Supreme, the songs and prayers
Of all create a harmony of purity

I have many mothers and fathers
My people have emerged from the discordancy
Of creation to a journey of one thousand moons and suns,
And a thousand more to where the great river,
The place to paddle meets the great waters,
From there on trees and lash though many perished
And were lost they found the Land of the Sun
I have rarely heard Guarionex speak so much

About himself, and yes, dear reader, you again
Are right, the speech fell on unresponsive ears
This modest man bragging about parentage
Was of little interest to the warring clans
Even when spoken as a god
I suggested to him another strategy
Which we would future use to great advantage
Guarionex commenced again to speak
Of Caridad and I broke in and said
"And in carrying him, she showed him
The secrets of the deep and of the sky"
(As an eternal spirit I can easily change
My shape and appearance
And I lengthened my legs about a foot
So I seemed to be tottering on stilts)
Keeping them in suspense about
Whether or not I would fall on my face
As I spoke, having captured their attention,
I also chased away the carrion birds
That were feasting on their dead
Thinking that showing such respect would
Further place me in their good graces
And attention, I later was told that was the way
They had of disposing of their dead, thinking that they
Would find their rest in the sky and actually were amused
By such attempt of mine, an impossible task
Of defeating the natural, immutable state of things
Such as carrion birds feeding on the dead,
I guess many of my clever turns of phrases
Were not so funny as I thought, and they were laughing
At me and not with me—yes, dear reader,
Even in your ignorance, you know
It is important to be aware of friends' and enemies'

Culture and beliefs before you try to help them,
I continued and said, she gave him
The friendship of the fish and birds
And knowing of their tongue, she left him on the shore
Where Yumac found him,
As a child he frolicked and spoke
With fish and bird on land and sea
And some say that great eagles would snatch him
For days to aerie crags and feed him tender morsels
Oysters, urchins and sweet berries
O dear reader, I know that even now you are scoffing
At the tale I tell, how I delight in your
Ignorance and disbelief, you think
That Stone Age man and woman would believe such
Stories of other men, and never modern man
But this is how I introduced Guarionex, many times,
In new lands, the clans knew this was of my invention
And for their amusement, why do you think they had
So many tales of gods and goddesses?

Guarionex, amused, would laugh
Uproariously at some hyperboles and also prance
Like a bird with neck stiff and bobbing head
Swim like a fish, and with flapping arms bob and dive
Or smash a mighty unseen axe into the trembling earth
The children would follow him, improvise of him and of the fish
Or the flying walking birds and crawling snakes
The lumbering tortoise brought the most laughs
How many bird eggs did Guarionex carry in his mouth to
Bury in the sand and then crawl as a tortoise into the water?
Taking my cues from their reactions
I would invent the most absurd and detailed tales
Of mirth and foolishness evoking convulsive laughter

Even from those that thought to laugh unseemly
The stories would end in general revelry
And a declared day of feast and dance proclaimed
With many slaughtered animals
Though not fish or birds, and many tales of troubles,
Adventures and problems of the clan

Not one voice was ever heard
In denial of Guarionex's parentage, nor of
His rescue by Caridad, but many said
They had known of her many acts,
And received of her support

And some wise men and women, even children
Remarked that in my eyes and voice they saw
Such great love for Guarionex
That they knew that in my heart was belief
That he in deed was a god, and if not all things
Were true, they could have been
His immanence inspired awareness
Of divinity in the world
And they treated him as godly personage
For his manner was such that
Evoked respect and admiration

Had Praxiteles such a model
He would have exceeded his Hermes
Guarionex's athletic aspect, his carriage
And his grace made my hyperbole
Seem but simple possibility

Though on this first essay on play
We succeeded in some amusement

We were told that Mother and Father would
Have to approve our remaining here
And second the purpose of our voyage
Which we had not dared unclothe
To steal away the Tree of Life
Or concupiscent branch from which
A full tree would bloom
For such a deed would grant
Eternal Life

MOTHER AND FATHER OF THE RACES OF HUMANKIND

Plaited palm leaves singly bound
Along the side, more generously
Bound at the roof to keep out
The rain made up the bohio
Where Mother and Father
Had lived and given life to the
Races of humankind

A grove of coconut palms extended all round
And a large pot on stones encasing
An extinguished fire exuded a sweet smell
Of an intoxicating palm toddy, some last
Remaining dregs which Guarionex
Tasted on his fingertips and passing
A wooden effigy holding a finely milled
Powder, he sniffed therefrom

Stepping from the glaring sun
Guarionex slowly entered the shaded entrance
And peered inside, in greeting

Singing the song of waking birds
As they argue and discuss who is to lead
And to where for the morning's repast

Inside, a mountainous man sat,
Cragged as a displaced boulder
Crosshatched with age, with
Flowing gray beard swirling
As surf breaking and spraying
Particles of wind and rain
On a rocky shore
Whorled to three tendriled
Branches over a protuberant belly
And next to him, and as imposing,
A woman with flaking skin
As a leaf-covered forest floor
Of forgotten aeons and long
White hair that wrapped
Around the two to provide
Warmth and modesty, ending
Carelessly splayed to the entrance
Upon which Guarionex walked

Hanging on the wall were many
Woody capsules holding clusters of
Triangle-shaped nuts, their shells,
The color of Mother and Father's skin,
Littering the floor
So as Guarionex stepped on them
His exclamation of pain waked the couple
Or at least made them stir as he could see
No open or staring eyes

Guarionex proceeded slowly
Moved by their great age
They had come unto this life
When the world spun around the sun
Much faster and humankind did
Twice the work in half the time
And the world extinguishing
In failed foray for humankind
The wise left for beyond the edge
And unwise stayed until their
Imaginings undid their humanness

As the world filled with
The uncertainty of errant thoughts
And dreams, Mother and Father
Were called to fill with deeds and loyalty
The eternal cleaving of one to
The other, and populating
Again with purer souls

Guarionex said in prayerful tones,
"Mother and Father, have you no rest?
You labor beyond your time
Your offspring no longer
Minister to you"

Upon these words as if the Earth
Had whelped a long-contained
Mass of pain and ire
The very foundation cracked
A whipsaw motion stretching
To the distant mountain range
A thunder roar emitted by
A wounded lion

Mother and Father moved and stirred
Threw off the motionlessness
Of a thousand years
"Who speaks?" the man exclaimed
And Guarionex was filled with fear
"Do not fear", the woman said,
"Father means no harm, but
To free you into the world
As I freed you from my entrails,
In which you were, comfortable, warm,
Content to live your life without the world
Exempt from destiny, but overtaken by
A simple destiny not conceived by you,
It is a simple death to be born,
And now again no destiny
Of your ken or thought, still wrapped
In ignorance without death until
The Earth expires"

"Will today bring my death, Mother?"
Asked Guarionex, "No", she said,
"Only at the end of eternity
For you like us
Were weaned on tenchweed and
Will see the way and the
Circumference of all things
Death brings birth and birth new sight
But loss of understanding and destiny"

"What is my destiny, Mother?"
"You will not know", she replied
Father interjected,

"Your destiny only to lose the way"
And here hope clouded the mind
Of Guarionex, and he exclaimed,
"I will know my destiny
I will find the way of my life"
"But enough, child", Mother said,
Father exclaimed, irritated, "Why
Do you awaken us to perception
Of this world when we would
Have slept until the next?"

Mother exclaimed,"Though unsaid,
He seeks eternity, for the way
May be found only on the fork
That leads to forever, beyond even
The eternity of this great universe"
I knew then that we were lost
And pulled Guarionex's arm
Beckoning to leave before
We paid the greatest price
But he refused as still in trance

Guarionex could only speak
The truth to them, and said,
"I have come to carry away the
Tree of Life, to build the heart of the
Fortress of my city, the city is built
Of the earth mixed with the rain of my land
The Tree of Life and the fortress
Will reach to heaven
And connect the world and
City with the sky and heaven eternal

But these men and women
Sprung from the body
Of your love, one for the other,
Interfere in their eternal war
Of sun, moon and stars"

"The black man and woman say
They are divinely chosen for
They worship the Tree of Life
Which is of the sun
The sun brings warmth and brings
All to grow, and is divine for
What it does in day"

"The yellow man and woman
Worship the Tree of Life because
It lives under the moon and it is
At night that the tree blesses
The Earth and all its creatures
In all their multiplicity
And is divine for it lives in Night"

"And the white man and woman
Worship the Tree of Life for the stars
Of the night and the stars that sail
Across the waters of the cosmos
Day and night,
And they say that in
The drawings of the stars you
May read the wishes of the gods
And in the burning stars that cruise
The heavens they inscribe the truth
Upon the sky and upon the Tree of Life

Their truth inscribed
In the veins of its leaves"
Dear reader, your humble scribe reminds
Each one has a story to die for

Guarionex concluded,
"Thus humankind fights, argues, separates
Tears down what the other builds
So none prospers"

Father said, "These are our children
And of this manner have always been
You would build a city and think
This strange?"

Mother in kindly voice and nod of head
Said, 'Take that dry branch of the
Tree of Life, plant it by that
Batata patch, to replace what you
Would take and your desire
Will be yours, eternity to beyond eternity
Of humankind, to the forever of presence
Of the One Supreme that lives in all
Eternities though they number
The grains of sand"

"And you will have wisdom to find
The way, but careful, do not pinch
Yourself on its thorns, for then the
Worse and best of your desire
Will be your regret"
My eyes said, Don't!
But I could not move

The branch was partly rooted in
The dirt floor, and Guarionex
Startled, it would not come
As he first pulled
He quickly went outside and
Planted it by a batata plant
Mother inspected his hand
When he returned and said,
"You heal quickly but that
Red drop by where the branch
Was rooted tells the tale
You have the best of your desire
And will still live beyond eternity
And the worst is also yours, you will
In body and soul die many times
Along the way and many swaths
Of time will be obscured
In dark wakelessness until
You hear your name"
Better he had never been born
But Guarionex seemed pleased
And at ease (Mother gave him
The bark of the jayabacana
To cure his finger)

"And the Tree of Life is mine,"
Guarionex declared, Father intoned,
"Of course my son, but you must
Convince the races of man to stop their wars
And freely bestow the Tree of Life to you"

THE HUMBLE SCRIBE SPEAKS OF GUARIONEX, THE LAST OF HIS NAME

Guarionex
His destiny to be born too many times
His way a broken road
A presence in mortal time
With sleep of centuries
The One Supreme's great joke
To achieve awareness of self and soul
We must sin of both,
The timid and blameless have no place in Paradise
Guarionex, a warrior of care and nurturing
Armed with a sword that cleaves
Falsehood from Truth,
Cleaves his own heart one part from the other
Now death impends, wakes him to birth

Reason is a wave that breaks upon a stony shore
Impelled by universal stress and force
Gathering each part with the other
Toward an implacable thrust,
In gathering, gathers too much forward
Movement, unsustainable height
Weight and space breaking
On shore, its oneness dissolved
To a shallow liquid spray that turns
To mist and air, tendrils leeching into the sand
Reaching, parting one from other
Ending in pools where captive fish feed

GUARIONEX APPROACHES THE RACES OF HUMANKIND

And now your humble, most-derided scribe
Must cast a net of words to bridge the gap
From scene to scene, Guarionex
Heeding not my words stepped out
Among the now warring clans
One group with fanlike arms of
Scythe-armed men in circular movements
Harvesting the souls of men, and the other
In encircling masses piercing their defense
With upraised spears that hung draped bodies
Like rags to dry, and the third (who
Later would be of fame called Javiteros)
From great distances, enabled by a throwing stick,
Launching javelins that impaled one or two
Unlucky souls, like necklace beads through heads
Or guts, no word of color here for this is of
The Sin of Men and not of race

Guarionex, his soul possessed by peace and truth
Calmness confronting death wantonly bestowed,
Did not speak but all three clans turned on him
And he flew as Iris is said to fly from the hand of Zeus
Avoiding all their efforts with the wiles of speed of
The birds and fish, and animals of the plains
Until, cornered, he dove into the sea
With dolphin's grace and with one breach and dive
His legs now fins sought darkest sanctuary

My grief unconsolable was not assuaged
With sentinel saguaro loyalty, I stood with arms upraised
With dark spines warding off all approach
And fruit that scorched the throats of men

Day followed day as my eyes searched the sea
Until soledad and loss replaced my grief
And time passed with the beat of generations
And I, accepting death, knew that only
The One Supreme could call him back

GUARIONEX FOLLOWS THE CALL TO THE DEPTHS
The water was silky warm and green, then blue
Then heavy as black honey which pushed back
With every stroke, then silence, eternal,
Forgotten unperceived

"I woke without name nor words,"
Guarionex recounted, "Nor history,
a desire for no thing, an otherworldly
Peace that belonged not to flesh,"
Guarionex! Guarionex! Awake!
I have awaited you, I am all you have desired
As you are mine, awake to my embrace

ROOMS OF GRACE
Perdida lived in many rooms,
Some of underwater mansions with
Stalagmite columns that supported the seas as canopies
The rumbling passage of scavenging fins
Could be heard against the walls;
Other rooms on open plains of
Unending unexplored vistas
She and Guarionex traveled them
And marveled at the varied beasts that fed
On the abundant grass and those

That preyed on them with claw and tooth
From sky or subterfuge of brush, night or speed
Still other rooms drifting on clouds
Or not distinguished from
The shape and form of clouds
The mighty eagles would fall to their grief
In trying to reach these mighty aerie retreats
From here Guarionex could see
The flow of time from start to end
The battle with the keepers of the winds
The dust kicked up by the journey
Of Guarionex, the first of his name,
The sins and pains of Guarionex, the builder of cities,
Yumac, the land of the sun, Maria and the ancient one
All eternally in a passage that would never end
And his many deaths were also revealed
All but his destiny splayed out on the face
Of Time and Earth, but he would forget
And forget that he had forgotten all,
Even the final battle with the ancient enemy

And their love blossomed
Not as startling revelation
Or act of fate, nor the finding of
A treasured destiny finally revealed
Nor magic consonance of harmony and souls
But as a deep pool from which both
Had always sipped, a familiar tie of flesh,
As though conceived by the same thought
Of the One Supreme, no miracle name,
But as one may say that is a tree and
That's the earth it's rooted in
So that look, or thought of one or other,

Or accidental touch of hand, or chores
Together, fetching water or scrubbing floors,
Inspired the same release and ecstasy
As the creation of a new universe
In dissolute joining
Such is the nature of being
That its greatest beauty, its most
Desired peace and destiny would enslave
Us to irrelevancy more stoutly than
The cleverest stratagem of
The ancient enemy, and with the
Passing of decades Guarionex
Knew he must escape

GUARIONEX TO PERDIDA, NYMPH OF THE PYROSOMES

In previous lives our souls were intertwined
And we have met before in many times
As parent, child, betrothed
Of either sex or condition in life
Wisteria blooms eternally entwined
In passing points to future destiny

A lashing spitting storm
Of wave and wind, then calm
Followed by gala day inflaming
The fallen tinder of many days
Of growth and drought

Memories, fallen to disuse,
Dried, curling to brittle shards,
Crushing memories of my love

For you, and yet even
In death, waking to inflame
The touch of you, your lustered
Skin, your breath mixed with mine

There are spaces in this land
And shadows that shelter me
From my love for you
Your sweet murmurings wake me
As the wind rustles the trees
I lash my soul and heart to
Memories of hurts and fears
Of future sufferings
Against all contrivance
They fly free, suckling
To the sweet flow of your desire
Your words transformed to
Perfumed vapors of your
Night-mantled places

PERDIDA PLEAS
Stay, Guarionex,
Destiny is but life deferred
Lost in dreams you harvest illusion
And bypass the sweetness
Of love timely picked

GUARIONEX REPLIES
Unfinished today impels
Me to undreamt tomorrow
Loneliness calls, not fulfillment,

Illusion not to be resisted is
A verdant valley of wasteful dreams
Prescience of nothingness calls,
The One Supreme resides in
Yearning and nonfulfillment
For the world is but a shadow
And the sky never meets the sea

FOUND FRAGMENTS OF NOTES ON TREE OF LIFE THE HUMBLE SCRIBE DISOWNS

These notes
On well-weathered clay
Are not familiar to me
Though they are marked
As I do mark and are
Consonant in many ways with
Memory and the aforewritten story
Though from where their provenance
I cannot say:

As saguaro sentinel with growth of centuries
Awaiting Guarionex's return from his
Sepulchral sanctuary, I grew to see far
Beyond the sight of men and was entranced to count
The many suns and moons, and learning
The quadrants of the spinning stars,
How each shone with whispered message
Of heteromorphic possibility that
Presented paths of tears, and others of
Laughter with crisis strewn, and others
Still of peace, silence and loneliness

(Yes, dear reader, what you awaken with
Each morn), all these perhaps so captured my
Mind that in motion and role I noted
Guarionex's return, but sight and thought
Were elsewhere, and I faithfully carved
These notes, but recall not doing so

GUARIONEX FINDS THE CENTER OF THE WORLD

Riding a whirling wind past
Many rain-blurred lands,
Guarionex was brought it seemed
By chance to the island of the great tree
Where he hoped to find the timber for
His city and sailing ships seen in his dreams
But knew not how to build
On this voyage that he recounted in great detail
And I accompanied him
And can assure the reader of the
Accuracy of his recall (though
Apparently not totally of mine), which
Concords with mine except
In some instances of my helpful involve
At certain times of stress
A moon-shaped cove of white sand
Reached out as to embrace
The green glass shallow sea
The shore stretched level on both sides
Dotted with groves of palms and trees brought
On the eastern storms
That ravaged these lands each year
Inner wet lands supported large

Colonies of flaming-colored
Long-legged birds building mud nests
In your time, rarely seen, my dear reader,
Another sin for which you must contend
For centuries these flocks have disappeared
But soon, even in your time, one lone
Flying creature in announcement of
Rising dawn will wake Guarionex
From centuries of sleep to
Fulfill his destiny

And at a misty sun-hazed distance
A forest at the foot of sharp-coned mountains
At ocean's edge, the large space of sand
Ending in simple palm leaf dwellings,
Surrounded by rolling hills
Seemed an arena, a space for pageantry,
And in that space, three groups of men
Contended, one group in chains of ten
As a spinning wheel of human spokes
The center being a green carved belt
Of stone as a giant yoke for man or beast
Another group in three phalanxes
As spear points to penetrate, dislodge
The wheel and its spokes, and a third
From distant purchase hurling spears
With throwing sticks, the battle raged
Until we put ashore

THE MEETING...
Parts of these tablets are very eroded
One can only assume that Guarionex

Introduces himself
A warrior exclaims:
Now we know who you are
We are the ones who will
Impede your task
We protect the great tree
And all its brood, and know your
Search for eternal life
Those that evade our axes will directly pay to
The spirit of the tree that steals the soul
Of those that would steal its brood
With that they fell on Guarionex
My being an eternal spirit is of great
Advantage in situations such as these
Moving back three steps I evanesced
By refracting light to the sides
And taking the appearance of
An empty tortoise shell, I sat at
A perfect vantage point upon which
To observe and take my notes; after all,
Cowardice is the better part of discretion

Guarionex moved fast with all the movements of birds
And creatures of the land and sea
As a tortoise digging her nest to lay her eggs
He sprayed sand upon their eyes,
As a snake in sideways motion he slid
Under their steps, as a bird he hopped from side to side
Missing their fists and stone-point axes
He even seemed to fly in great leaps until
They linked their arms surrounding him
As Guarionex leapt, escaped and ran
They set the wheel of many axes to spin

In solitary pursuit, some ran after him
Up and down the great arena
By mountain and sea
But Guarionex's steps were so swift
He left no marks upon the sand
And even ran upon the water
As a winged creature catches the wind
And finally outrunning a hundred men
One by one, and tiring, hemmed in,
He turned to the open shore
Dove in and like the denizens of the deep
Submerged and was not seen again
Again much is missing and illegible until...

GUARIONEX OF THE PYROSOMES
All the generations of the races of
Humankind passed away, one by one,
And arose again to slaughter each,
And at the vertex of the sun, covered in grime
And gore would rest and together lunch
With mild ripostes as family day
Of feast, Mother and Father
Rarely heard, never leaving their shelter,
But at evening time when the keening cries of
Children's grief were heard, deep rumbling
Wails would emanate from where lived
The ancient pair

The saguaro garden grew, many root
Sproutlings growing large, encroaching
On the shore, freeing part of it from
Battle and blood, the oldest one,

Growing to the height of many men,
All with arms upraised as in beseeching prayer
Or in horror of so many bloody deaths

Sun's white-hot summits beyond count
Nature's implacable expression of dominance
Extinguished, as if a vandal's brush of hot black honey
Or the blackdamp that flows from
The earth and feeds the fires of the plains
Had been painted across the burning orb
And then splashed and stretched, and poured
Over the sky and clouds encasing all in dark
The fires of the meal illuminating the whites
Of their eyes, nothing else could be seen,
Until even these were pulled into the dark
By a malevolent hand, a fiend has pulled out
My eyes, yelled one, but then all were
Imprisoned in the silence of their fear of death

After each had suffered, in his heart and mind,
The most fearful deaths a dozen times, they saw
A swimming light, leaving trails of spotted
Shining bits, a fragment of fallen sun or moon?
A fiery leviathan of the deep here to take their souls?
A walking flame in shape of man, a messenger of the sun?
I knew by shape and walk, his head held high,
Guarionex returned from a death of centuries
I heard his name, Guarionex, a refrain
Of the wind using the tendriled leaves
Of palms as tongue, he walked as bright
As the sun, but illumined only in self
And the rest remained impenetrably dark
Even I, an eternal spirit, had heard of but

Never seen a soul called forth from eternity
As if he sensed my thoughts, he turned to me
And said, "Spine filled sentinel, come down
To earth, now turn your vigilance to our concerns
Gather your abandoned tablets and carve
My words, no zealous pronouncements
Of sun-god deeds, this fiery covering
But well-rubbed pyrosomes, loyal minions
Of Perdida, and extinguishment of sun
And light but the snuffing of their souls
By weight of sin, when man's course
Is steered by self, he cannot see the world
My sins bigger still, condemned me to eternity
A grief surpassing blindness"

GUARIONEX LEAVES BEHIND THE TREE OF LIFE

I surrender to the nature of humankind
And will request no more of you
Punishment sufficient unto eternity
To revenge and dominance chained
And as he spoke the black damp melted
From the sky, and the Earth, at first
Grayly lit, brightened from his every word
I have tasted the fruit of the Tree of Life
Seeking transformation and to shed
The grief of the journey through this life
Marked by the milestones of Soledad
And violence one upon the other
And my own sins have brought me
Death and Life, Loss and Love,
In eternal married bliss

And so with our voyage ended
And the world from which we came
Lost now in the mists of time
We strove toward the future
In a quickly assembled raft

GUARIONEX, BRAVE NOBLE LORD, THE LAST OF HIS NAME, RETURN VOYAGE TO THE LAND OF THE SUN

Enduring with fevered strength the tide
And wave, reaching for where the sea
Meets the sky but never catching the edge
Which fled with increasing speed,
I came upon another land, a mirror
To our world, but filled with women
So fair I lost all care for home

One bore me eight children,
Each more beautiful, quick of action
And grace than the one before
I clove to her seawater and coconut smell,
Which woke my tongue,
Engorged my throat, and wrenched my breath
In great gasps, unquenchable lust,
Turning mute as the white-striped
Leviathan devours swimming masses
Of flesh and unsated, swims endlessly
Hunger and need, a numbing mad desire
Devoured all memory of
My ancient home

All intent, remembrance and acts
Fell upon themselves, gone, subsumed
Into the other, and joy became
The taste of the other feeding greedily
Upon the detritus of passions spent
An albatross riding a capricious wind,
Water rising to a palm's crown,
A wave that mounts and swells to cloud the sky
But does not break, until a storm
Of flame and wind rips the crest
Across the shore and rocks
Such is the woman who comes to me
Now in the ending of all I see
And before each breath I taste her in my throat
I could not leave where humankind
Neither worked nor cared but gathered
Heaven's bounty with outstretched hand
Days passed, blended with moons and years,
My heart asleep but to lust and ease,
Lost all thoughts of home

Sun-drenched days and rain by night
Weighed down the trees with fruit
Grass bore succulent pearls of sweetened grain
That in sweet repose, in womb of sun's embrace,
One might but reach that these may fall
In fragrant sensual bursts cooling the skin
To wipe away worldly deception and illusions,
Filling one with amusement of fearful destiny
In sleepless dreams of lonely pleasure domes
Of sky and wind and deepest ocean caves
By scalding currents carved

From where the thought, I cannot ascertain,
Perhaps a lightning strike that lit the night
But with intent to bring my clan to live
In this land of careless repose, I took my craft
And drifted effortlessly and was borne again to
My ancient home; I did not know
I had been called to fulfill my destiny and
Slipped to this hard-edged world,
Which one a dream?

One hundred moons had passed, or more
But when the craft hit ground, I awoke from
My dreamless dream, and either rose to light
Or fell from sky, to where wave and behemoth
Had brought me as a child
And now prefer to stay where work in day
Is followed by night-darkened dreams of strife,
Death and unsteady flying glides from mountaintops

CHAMBERED MEMORIES

Half encased in nearby fossil coral reef
And grainy sandstone rock, an ancient
Ocean bed, pushed up to rain, wind and tide
By mighty continents' compression
A chambered ammonite shell
Its outer shell washed away, edges rounded,
The many chambers polished by the surf,
Exposed, caught my eye,
Had this been here before my clan
Had ever walked these shores,

And I who knew each rock,
Each she-crab, and all her crablings,
Even to seven generations,
Had never seen nor counted its many rooms?

The shell revealed gracefully formed
Pearl-chambered rooms to serve as an abode,
And each, more than ten, and yet again,
And another ten, sealed off
But to memory's call
As the architect, a worm divine,
Palladio's kin ten million years removed,
Moved on to more spacious ones

Though then unschooled, your humble
And modest scribe has since learned much
And knows the readers well and their pretense
And just as you see us through darkling lens
More as spirits than flesh of your
Imprecise imaginings, fantasies
Of your need to wash away regret,
Do we see through lens's protuberance
Into your daily lives, your shape and gifts,
And send well-wishes to transcend our sins

Ancient shell, what is your count
Of days and Earth's spin?
Time has eroded your sleep below
The sand, lava flows and silting sister shells
Great and small, the ocean is
The winding of the master clock
Slipped into the waistcoat of the stars

Sewn with dust and filament of lights,
And the clouds hourglasses of dripping rain
That falls and wears away these walls
Our hopes and dreams to leave devoid
The chambers of our thought
In these rooms, celebratory balls were held
To mark great days, or vernal equinox,
Or sun's ascent or completion's end
But joy's leavings are gone and only
Doubt or emptiness remains,
This chamber, was that when love first came
Or this when love had left
And that when never there,
Or does the wind and surf wear away,
Erase our sins, our grief, regrets
And evil we have caused
So these now-tainted rooms
Spare us from blood and pain
The faces, names of our deceit
The strings of misfortunes
That fall on those betrayed
The murmur of falling rain,
The pulling pushing surf,
The work of tides, a whispering wind
That wears away all that clings
To a ceaseless moving world
Metronome of Earth's spin
And long-arcing traverse of Sun's path
Across the void bringing in its wake
Our games of thought, discoveries
Of what already is, has been
And on its way to what is its end

What secret talks were held
In these iridescent rooms?
Remembrance, all is gone
What matters Earth's groaning faults and rifts
Pushed in or out by moon or sun
Accordion of the heavenly stress
And shove, notes and choir's roar,
Deep bass sounds at mantle's core
Piercing wind notes of rushing storms
Through mountain passes,
And rising prayers of fluttering leaves
And beating wings, the modulating beat
Of tides and waves, the crescendo
Of work and toil, the screams of grief and joy
In humankind's advance, is this
Unfinished symphony to be muted
As we go to where you lead, sacred worm?

Who would count today, upon endless yesterdays
Or hope for a tally of days to come
Without hope of meaning retrieved
And remembered joy or love to live again
In ecstasy, a river of unending now,
A Sun-piercing flock of rising todays
Singing full-throated notes of color
Against a crimson sky but to announce
The joy of what has been lost?

Is memory then time, but how remember
If time brings but an empty room,
Meaning must be for remembrance
And remembrance to count one day

Against another one or then all days
Would be but one, what meaning
In these empty rooms, why move
From small to large and seal one
From other one and rob the self
Of enjoyment of labors past
What meaning give to a faceless worm
That builds a treasure as simple house
Something Croesus could not have done
With all his gold and that perdures
Through universal time while humankind's
Greatest monuments decay
Even as the cornerstone is set?

Where is there evidence of this formless face?
Not in these sweeping swirls, and voluptuous
Rounded forms nor in silent rooms
Where dwelt divine architect
Where is meaning now?
If there is no trace, then it was not there
Only wind and tide remain,
They keep their metered pace
Subject to counts of sun and moon,
Only obscured by the rain's fall

The story of star's demise
Sun's extinguishment
Is but one note of an unfinished symphony
Heard only by the One Supreme
Who rises then to start the day
At the end of time unspoiled
Man's action takes place in memory
Despoiled by slow decay,

Misplaced intent, not held in thrall
By all that can be seen,

The One Supreme's loving gaze
The fluid we call time
That sustains the world, all things,
In pendant form, one beat, the first,
And then goes on to creation's ecstasy,
Universal working gravity, and celestial orbs,
Or insect's eggs upon a leaf

Not meaning, face nor love is there
In your empty rooms, One Supreme remains
But seeing to other things,
And I, Guarionex, remain but will not last to see
You freed by wind and tide,
Ground down to grains of sand,
The end of my earthly days is close
And though acclaimed a hero and a god,
I will be cast as ash upon these shores
And come to rest, wash inside
Your empty chambers soon
When will Time begin again for you
Or has it stopped eternally as soon it must for me?

What formless worm spun this
Surpassing grace of all our architecture?
Did it possess an inner dream,
Or was it the humble vessel of divine thought?
Our dreams set the stars to spin, expand,
Contract and whirl to darkness lost
From this dreamlike state of thought
Comes metered life, meaning, remembrance, faith, belief,

Which drive the worm to build these empty rooms
To hold its dreams and survive to this day
But disappoints for all is gone but intent

THE HUMBLE SCRIBE SPEAKS OF HUMBLE VESSELS IN THE LAND OF THE SUN

Land like this gave rise to gods
Not divinely sent,
Nor achieved by miracle
But humankind of simple deeds
That wrench the world aside from destiny.
To whom did it occur, which woman
Gave her life for love of child
Or captured, tended fire fallen from the sky
Which man to tame the beasts
Or pledge his love to woman?

These humble vessels
Of the One Supreme's Word and Hand
In smallest ways, gods working simple-seeming deeds,
That set our destinies apart from
The grazing fields, and the tree's bitter fruit
Vessels worthy of Word and Hand
Working in the smallest of ways
In Grace divine, the fluid we call time,
In which we live and breathe
Rising seas nor wave of hand shape this world,
But by bidding wind to lift one grain of sand a year
Are mountain ranges raised and such is done with man,
These grains, the humble gods of home and hearth,
More dramatic ends invent

Than mountain ranges, burning stars,
Flooding seas, great abodes of kings

Who thought to weave or sail the wind?
And so it is household gods I seek
Who take silent care and vigil
Of small dimension and simple deeds
These will still shake the world with love,
When the tale of Guarionex is told
All I tell and write is true,
As true as sea and wind,
Earth and fruit and comes from
Such proof as this: that who we are
Could never be without
Such simple deeds as these

And those in cemis praised,
Mothers, fathers, heroes of love and deeds
Now household gods that protect,
That in their turn helped the tribe
Survive in fertility of mind and thought
All this, and more
From act and love, to meaning, memory
And then oblivion

All this was soon to pass

GUARIONEX AND THE BIRDS OF THE SEA

Many days passed and blended with moons and years
I filled my days and became the elder chief,
Solid and strong and broad, and my clan
Was called those who walk the beauteous land

Of sea and sun, a woman grieved at
My loneliness took me away
From worrying surf, I forgot the other lands,
Though strife and work marked my days
Joyfully I greeted each day
With work and sacrifice

Fountains in the sea, black glistening forms
White giant birds with beating wings
Upon the ocean's edge, announced with din and smell,
They flew with men upon their backs
Three ships came as clouds from
The edge of sea and sky,
Fear leapt to our hearts for gods only kill and maim
For selfish ends, but men for sport or pride
Extinguish all

The clan saw these men as gods
Upon the backs of swimming birds
And I to meet certain death
If I were to greet these gods,
Our ancestors, now returning
As gods or ghosts called back by naming them
With living things, I saw men,
Their circumstance and need, despair, content
Revenge and love, bloodthirst fear,
And resolved to challenge both men,
And gods, if that they be,
To nature's nobler course, and maintain
My choice and upper hand
By counting on gods' and men's
Prideful self-regard and blindness
To others' needs and my craft to weave

An account of deceit and greed
As last resort

For Guarionex was man and also god,
And had no fear to challenge both gods and men
His trips around the isle had taught him well
The need and lust for trade that all men have,
Even loved more than pillaging and rape,
Exhausting and dangerous chores,
That kill potential customers
The same ends are more calmly, safely met
By advantageous trade and exploitive use
Of gold and deceptive words of care
But these of the white bird ships
Only thought of gold and slavery
Not to build with care, preserve for
Future stability, the innocent they saw
As reason to kill and the humble to enslave
(And those among them more kindly
Leaning were deceived and removed)

I gathered the clan from where they hid,
Wooded hills and rocky secret coves,
And harshly spoke to more than few
Threatening, whipping some,
Recalled past favors due,
This danger surpasses all
Courage, I had, a reckless lack of fear
It so appeared, and dominion
Of plants, elements, and
Creatures of the sea,
In gentle sway, I had led my clan,
Convinced them to my view

But now not time for only gentleness
I harshly spoke:
"Ashore they'll come, be men or gods,
And finding neither gold nor food
Will eat our children and despoil
Our women, young and old"

Now fury gave birth to
A stranger within, harder than
The rocky coves, ravenous
And tearing as the hunters in the sea,
Implacable as ruthless huracan,
Through skin and tissue he smelled the blood
Of the creatures nearing his small isle,
And lusted to spill it in great rivulets
To feed the monstrous brood that would
Arise from blood-crazed deeds
And so it was, for before he spied
The white-winged flock, the winds
That had mightily pushed this brood
Had brought the stench of death and blood
That haloed their presence and honeyed with poison
Each word they used to lure and stun to passive assent
All that they would devour, he struggled to maintain
A gentle manner for he knew
This fury was the poison's work
And would but speed the end

Each of thirty men went out, to gather
Fruit, roots and game, one day and night
They worked by sun and moon's full glow,
While the ships of men approached
And readied now to land and kill
If need arose or not

As they went out to gather food
They prayed to all the gods
As they went out
For one hundred steps
They chanted full

"We are the land
That gives us strength"
Dispersing each prayed,
"Mother of this brown earth
That nestled us,
Yuca is my father
Mother, brother, sister too
The other yautia
And ñame too"

"Mother Atabey
Who gives with *caridad*
We are but a root
Conceived in earth, in you,
Stretching in moist earth
So we may drink we cling to you
Your womb
And refuse the light
We are your flesh
As are all living things"
I prayed, Mother Atabey,
Stir the winds, huracan
And the ocean's flow
Blow them back to where they came
But wind and water were calm

And the earth and surf whispered
To them and they knew,

This vine is only here since
My brother's birth
The mother vine is this,
You see its hanging gourds
The water cup I drank from
Birth came from her
My mother hollowed this one out
Like this, with this marking,
As only ones from this vine are marked
She dried it calling forth in dreams
What I would be
And filled it with fruit and water
For me to drink, another has sprung
Since my birth, clinging to
The bower's walls
My children have drunk
At birth as will their own

And knowing this
They knew all
Where all the fruit, roots
And game belong
And it is where they belong
That they may gathered be

Guarionex set his plan:
How set my foot, which star
To guide my steps
My heart sets valor upon itself
And girds itself with love recalled
Of landscapes full of blossomed love
And memories each in season coloring

And bearing fruit, my soul dispersed
In flowing ribbons of thoughts and joys
That touch the faces of all that
Live upon this land
Of love's reward upon the Earth
The tides, suns and moons
Of gathering food by the sea

My naked self,
Poor instrument, quaking
So I can hardly stand,
I loose my hair, the feathers fall,
I am at birth awaiting passage
To another world,
The shell I grasped, my amulet,
When found that night by
Kindly Yumac who placed it
With plaited grass around my neck,
I remove and swallow to take
With me to my destined end

Only the roundest and most fully formed of root,
And fruit, and fattest of the game were picked,
The rest in hidden caves were stored,
But yet ten full canoas were filled, piled high
To provision many months at sea
For the many men on the winged ships

I set out and tied prow to stern
Ten *canoas* filled with goods
Gliding on an outgoing tide
And knowledge of the currents

That tear from shore to sea
Once upon the sea I recognized
The path to its glorious end
Where all might live to their
Natural end, but no return for me
I soon approached the ships and
As I took a rope from the largest
All my clan leapt into the sea
And swam to shore
Except for two who stayed
From loyalty, one was run through
By a flowing scabrous horde of
Jabbering men and one was handed up
With me and all the goods we brought
I was quickly tied to a peeled leafless tree
And on his left the one who died, and on his right
The one who lived to serve as scribe
For all he said and did
To tell the tale of Guarionex, and that was I
Devoid of ancestors' names or guiding hands
What godless men were these?
They spoke in medley of many tongues
And understood each, I soon learned
All their tongues

For Guarionex had learned
All the ways the world and beasts converse
With men and gods;
The wind, rocks, sea and sky all speak,
To come together in calm or storm or colored sky
The birds at sunrise call as they awake
From their nesting caves along the shore
And spread to inner mountain slopes,
And from trees or backs of beasts

Or at water holes as they dive
To eat grass and bugs, they plan their day
And advise the fish, crabs, and fruit that day
How many of their number they need to eat
And what they will return in trade
So all may flourish, how much easier
To learn the tongues of hypocrisy and perfidy

The smell of rotting human waste
And flesh had hit from far away
And now the noise and chattering
Screams, no longer muffled by
The roiling surf, rose and fell
Upon my ears like a devil wind
Ripping sand and shore
Their tattered shirts and pants
Moving like thrashing snakes at war
Gesticulating men with
Slashing swords fell upon
The fruit and game, which quickly disappeared
Down below in grips of carrion beasts
Some did not descend
To eat in dark but fell
Upon the food and ate it raw

These were strong and agile men
But knew not this land
And many sorties had gained
Them but water, and narrow survival

The wild devouring men calmly spoke
The manner of my death
Considering not whether to kill
But how, to weigh with irons

And throw me to the sea
Or saving the irons, and skewering me
One frugal fellow thought
To butcher me as provision
For long return to home
My facial gestures, signs and few
Halting words I had quickly learned
Conveyed the latter might wisest be
But I would prefer to be set free
They appreciated my evenhanded objectivity
But were set upon their own ideas

And as they did intend to finish me
All were in silence struck, as the crabs and birds
On the night of my discovery,
From a darkened room emerged
An imposing shadowed man in red coarse weave
With threads of gold, his broad sword
Swinging on his hip, the hilt
Catching the sun's bright light

Now unseen, I slipped from the binding ropes
As smoke between the logs
Goes free to meet the sky
As in the familiar children's game that
I played at night's descent
After day of roving shore and fields,
Having set the fire we played
At binding each, as the Carib
Do to their captured slaves,
To see who could slip the tightest bonds

I was at the shadowed door in two quick bounds
Prostrate before El Capitan

With his foot he rolled me through
And closed the door in the darkened room
I heard soft-spoken tones as those I use
With my own clan, and movement to and fro,
As he entered, I saw the crowd dispersed,
And men engaged in many tasks
He lit a lamp and busied himself with
Some paged books and charts
From a darkened wall
A vision with a silvered glow emerged
That ripped a cry of joy and fear
There hung an image of the woman
Who had brought me to these shores

Guarionex did not remember that long-gone night
But through the years had formed a vision in his eyes
Of how she looked down as gently placing him
Upon the shore, and prayed that in his last day
She would come and as behemoth or woman fair,
Suckle him in sea-dark caverns,
Take him back to the deep
The day the elders shared the story of the clan
He went to the secluded cove
And carved her likeness
Upon a sea-scarred rock
Giving her a crown of sun and stars,
A smiling face gazing down in love
A gown that flowed as the currents of the sea
To swaddle an infant son
And a pedestal of the waves and moon
On that day as he worked
She whispered in the wind, the mist,
The first word love

And the names of all those that came from
First woman and man

Could this strange ship, could they be gods?
He had found her likeness and stood transfixed
In quiet joy, as though
The sun and moon within him shone
This seen by all, no man dared speak,
Nor touch as they quietly passed
Three days and nights
He neither ate nor drank
And did not sleep,
On the fourth,
He fell and slept

Awakened by the rising sun and birds' call
I explained to El Capitan that she my mother
Had placed me here, and I
Had carved her likeness on the rocky shore
Pan-demon-ium ensued, as some would have
Burned me at the stake and others
Would have worshipped me
Calm slowly gained some ground,
El Capitan resolved to visit, as he said,
Our Blessed Mother of the Rock
Had he a similar birth
And was my unlikely looking twin?
Each word of his set ten men to tasks
And we were quickly set upon the sea
Rowed by six of his strongest men
I pointed toward the hidden cove
And soon all were prostrate upon the shore
All voices in prayer strained

As the tide receded and threatened to strand us
Upon the shore, El Capitan arose and carved
On the rock base, *amador*, which meant
All those that loved the Blessed Mother
He said the word means love, or one that loves
The One Supreme and the Mother of All
I replied all our words mean love
But in different words and hues and forms,
As each blade of grass stands alone but is all one
El Capitan, the only one who understood
That as all things presence
The One Supreme
Every word rises from
The word for love

And so we returned, but most peculiar men
Of the white-winged ships, they speak of love
And praising love, but quickly turn to praise
Of gold and killing all in praise of purity,
And One Supreme
The next day's trip was to the clan's bower
And I to convince all to bring
Their gold, food, women and children to the ship

They came from similar climes and saw
These as virgin, fertile lands by war
And conquest theirs, as accustomed
From ancient times in their own lands
And who is this Guarionex who with
Open hand provisions us but hides
The gold and women too in mountain caves?

Belly full or not, these men treasured gold
And dreamt of gold and once
I haltingly described and conversed
In their many tongues of wondrous
Lands, to which this isle, Yumac's land,
Was but stepping-stone to gold-filled lands,
Easily hammered amulets of gold,
Sparkling rock, colored stones,
And seeds that grant godlike
Sleep and dreams, and where the beasts
Unbidden roll themselves on savory
Spices of the plains and leap onto the fire
To provide sumptuous meals for humankind,
And how water flows, sparkling pure
From mountain bulwarks of the gods
To give eternal life
They quickly thought to sail to where I led
Especially the one foreordained to return
In stubborn search for the waters
Of eternal youth
Being warned that the passageway,
Stayed closed a hundred moons
And opened only this short span,
One spring's awakening, and quickly closed again
We prepared to sail and I as guide
My life to forfeit if I lied

THE INNER LANDSCAPE
The inner landscape flows not with
Creation's riotous spring
Nor teeming stars and galaxies
But with silent forebodings,

The shadowed past, intention
And action accompanied by
Ephemeral ghosts in darkened halls,
Or as lava pulsing hot
Descending inexorable
Crusted cool and dark
But pulsing deep-falling
To blister, ignite
The most profound firmament
On which our selves depend

What mis-born, aborted souls are these
That birth a self as idol and god,
Reversing creation's natural flow
That enshrines soul as divine
The rest as detritus of life's travail,
A self that grows through plunder and strife
And sees the soul as mirrored twin
To grind and join
To worldly goals of greed?
Self will stalk the world and other selves
Until the one remaining self-supreme
Denying death and emptiness
Until the end of consciousness
Founds a terror reign
Of death for all we feed upon

Desire and greed the firmament
A golden bowl that bears fruit
Plucked too soon or too late decayed
With minor columns of hope and love
Bearing the weight of the world
And unsated natural love

That devours all
So humankind may
Shape desire to ruin
And hope released to enchain,
And despoil love and time,
And the presence of the One Supreme
To death and ownership

The end of my earthly days is close
And though to be acclaimed a hero
And god, the latter is not true,
But soon to come when men tell their tales
Of Guarionex
And I reside at the end
Of my starry flight

THE HUMBLE SCRIBE RECALLS
"All things will come to light,
To recall, what was and is and will be."
These were Guarionex's last words
Guarionex's face shone as he left
It gathered light from the sun
And at night the moon and stars
The firelight and the resplendent clouds
Guarionex's body every hue of dark and green and light
We saw him sail on those great birds
Looking back on his ancient home
Until from the ships, white full sails
Drowned in clouds at edge of sea and sky
Darkening to a deep blue of black
There shone a light as to touch the stars
And smoke arose,

Perhaps a cloud that flowed to us,
And in the days that came
I tasted him in the rain
And heard him, as was his way,
Softly speak of his father
In the rustling leaves of Yumac's tree,
I blew on the tendrils of the sea
To join with him as they encircled
The chambered ammonite in plunging
Bits of sand and silt caressing
The rounded forms he would gently swirl
With finger strokes saying
I ready my resting place

For many nights, the clan would come
To rest along the shore, staring outward
As if he might roll up again
In the beating surf, and told tales of how
He swooped and played with birds
And how he talked in whistles,
Whoops and trilling cries
The crane, song and humming birds
Would surround, follow him
Running, jumping as he, and taking flight,
Circling him, a rounding storm
That would lift him from rock to perch
At daybreak, the clan dispersed
And more each day were gone
Until it was only I who told the tales
And struggled to record these words
To memory

Guarionex was a man
Easily slipping in and out of sight

In body and joy, joining the roiling surf
In undulating forms, in movement and stroke,
Guarionex pranced and leapt
As birds in form and flight
On one leg or two, sideways cocked
And walked stiff-legged with bobbing head
His laughing cries, coloring the sky
In bright and middling blues, golds and reds

Slowly, the great pool of flesh
That fertilized this land
Since ancient times
Broke forth upon the world
And the last rivulets dried
Into the sky as passing mist
All was gone, the clan was gone
The birds flew to further coves
And to give them their fill
The crabs sunned themselves elsewhere
Their burrows filled with sand

The land became darker still
With coarsened grass, leaves
And widening, reaching trees
Varying climbing and nesting vines
Circled, dressing their trunks
Forcing the canopy to spring
Toward the sky to reach the light
The earth created a mantle of trees
And vines, enriched with fallen leaves,
Unpicked fruits and seeds
To sleep in peace, awaiting
Guarionex

And now the end,
On that last day he said to me:
I see the dark and light of the mountains
Beyond the beating wings
Of my words, the bursting color hue of
The sea's profoundest depths
Profess my love for you
And my ancient home
I trill untiringly in the birds'
Ringing notes of loneliness
That shatter my bones,
I grind the rocks with my wrath
And mix a slurry soup of tears and sea
To drink and shape my ancestors' progeny
To compose my words, limbs and thoughts

I see my destiny clear from the first day
Of creation to now and beyond
The world throbs with clarity
As it dissolves, a dream,
I now recall I had forgotten all
And am yet to complete the great
Circle of my destiny and will return
As the One Supreme recalls my name
All things will come to light
To recall, what was and is and will be

BOOK 7

MARIA DREAMS OF GUARIONEX

GUARIONEX RETURNS
I hear my name, I now awake
Though I, Guarionex,
Spirit I have become
A man I am in all but flesh
No glimpse or hold of destiny
Enslaved to serve in this crowded world
I who have served once as man,
Am now an observing god to her
Only a god can span a sleep
Of five centuries and awake
To city made of stone and tar
Filled with the hordes who brought
To misery and loss those that walked
The beauteous land of sun and sea
And burnt my body upon the sea
As scribe I will record her many trials
For those today that search for selves
Accommodating to passing needs
And find no center upon which to spin
Suffering moves humankind to change
And well-observed resolves
To thoughts and acts that alleviate

Wake now, Maria, to your dreams
I have been sent to observe,
Not impinge nor interfere
In your destiny, but dreams
Are ghosts that rising
Evanesce to vague recall
I will set them down for all
To see, and accompany,

To where you would go
If the One Supreme grants me
Substance and shape,
With love to light your way
My destiny delayed
For this cannot prepare
The Sun's final resting place unless
The beast has sent two angels
As bright a pair as moon and sun
To entice and turn your gaze
To earthly paradise and then
Shatter all to cymbal fanfare
And stop the universal melody

MARIA AWAKENS IN EVENING'S YESTERDAY
A strong autumn sun
Breaks now into her
Aerie nook, and brisk winds
In patterns blow
Red, brown leaves down the streets
Of concert halls, restaurants,
Book and clothing stores
All things desired

Fused by the cool night air to the marbled halls
And warmed by rising sun
Music notes are loosed in riffs
Of symphonies of many years,
Echoes of Valkyries, lovers spurned, pastorales,
Books spill from sidewalk stalls
Unwind in streaks of many-colored tales
That wrap around as low-flying clouds

And shred to words that fall
As snow to burst above
The ground in deconstructive fury
Of all that's sense
In words too light to sink,
Too dense to vaporize
But stroked by vertiginous winds,
As winged ideas, some catching on
Clothes of passersby
And flowing, through strawberry fields,
As opalescent fog of inconclusive thought
That then's resolved by bright daylight
To saffron flags
For sake of gaiety

Maria of rounded forms
Compact, with black and curly hair
Moves in measured pace
To the shifting flowing world
The counted days, fallen leaves,
Next spring's buds, passing cars,
Pale Male's rise and swoop,
The background shudder of moving things
Echoed in her step and gaze
Steps now across the pink-veiled
Dawn of day that chased
By the searing sun flees
To overtake the night,
Emerges as color-striated
Evening of yesterday

The four winds whisperingly
Shape the words she hears

In their passage sheared by the gray square
City spires, great stalks upon a plain,
And striking high and low notes,
As musical accompaniment
To the winding back of the world

To a time when the waters
Created neither chaos, nor disharmony
And rose in mighty walls, or fell becalmed
Feeding all in dreamy satisfaction
Spawning the face of the One Supreme
In myriad shapes and forms,
Of rock, fire and sky
Tendrils of the spoken words
That named all things to give them form
These less dust than water

Where then do I take my stand, she thought?
Without wings or fins,
Words swept away,
Not borne by the throat of the world
Pinned between the earth and sky,
Heavy of step with background songs of loss
And blasphemy, in dread
Of encroaching seas

I too may name and shape,
Not hard and formful things,
Nor life,
But shapes unseen,
Dreams undreamt,
Of the poised, intended thought
Of One Supreme to speak my name

THE FIRST ANGEL APPEARS
The first angel, wrapped in majesty
Of stance and unworldly light, then spoke:

What great hearts comprehend suffering
Yet do not descend to pain's decease
And drift as mist, in elegant shrouds of sky,
Trailing a flame-driven wind,
Desire in drunken sleep,
Toward days of no surcease?

What great minds live
In splendored diversity
Thriving in the poisoned wake
Of thought and intention
Witness to the celestial workings
Of an infinite god
Still in the birthing madness of desire and joy
Yet give to death new forms
And greed new depths
In the fruits of life planting new rebellions
That tear apart understanding?

What great voices now speak
To truth in lies
Call to light in darkened depths,
To breath in profoundest sea
Their words to conquer not submit to truth
Each word colored feathers of the sky,
Scales as sequins of the sea,
Pelts from the creatures of Eden,
Hammered chiseled golden leaves
And colored stones even from

The breast of the Earth
As a mantle to dress as gods?

Power you must seek
To bring God's rule upon the Earth,
Seek power's exercise
And change the world for good
To see your own advance
The world's corrupt and will destroy
Through wile and might all you attempt
Unless power flows to your self
And through weight of gold and influence
Honeyed words of love and politic
Develop weight accrete great strength
And shape and hammer all things
To your design

MARIA'S REPLY TO THE FIRST ANGEL
In a child's game of swings at night
Sweeping in smooth arcs
To weightlessness at apogee
Where climb nor fall exist,
But weightless hesitation
I am the still of the sky
And grasp the moon and stars
Belonging nor duty to none
Cracking the silent night
With great wings, a swooping owl,
Talons stretched and beak, fully me,
Not mine nor anyone's self

The breeze with flowers' scents,
The rain's descent, no shadows

Of the past, nor future's pull,
Only the world's acceleration,
The moon's pull, the sun's speeding drive
Pulling its weighty brood
Of rocks and gas,
I freely live my fantasy
And dream fullness

My smell, my words, my laughter thrown
Inscribed as puzzles in the sky
My tears as waves of the sea
My breath the night's stirring flight,
My hips the mountain's shapes
My hair galaxy filaments
Strung together as cloth of my own design
To shield me even from the One Supreme
Or round Us both in a swirling tent
In nothingness to play in dreamlike prayer
That We are alone

I, Guarionex, witnessed this,
The first angel disappointed
Withdrew and conferring with
The second, in form of most beauteous man,
Fairer than any womankind
Yet sinewy and strong
(The beast in supreme
Maliciously wise intent had sent
Australians) urged him to seduce

THE SECOND ANGEL OFFERS LOVE
The second angel, hirsute, but as
Just emerged from ancient marble stone

With eyes that reflect all that woman
Seeks and tenderness, sweetly sings:

The first word was song
Carried by a river of dreams of you
Spilling splintered light that fixed
In the heavens as stars

A word sung as praise of you
Brought Earth as fixed firmament
A cry the beasts
A sigh lonely man

In silence that shames
All music invention
In modesty created
You have come to leaven
My pain with love
Come to me

MARIA'S REPLY TO LOVE
If I could find myself
Wandering alone in the world
A hungry battered self
Abused and raped
Third born, though delivered first,
A weight on all the hopes of family
A blight to be sold or used
To support, advance the hopes
Of all the rest

If I could find myself,
An empty haggard soul

Eyes downcast, flinching at
Sudden moves of any hand
If I could find myself,
Such pained company
Would be all I need
I would no longer feel ashamed
Or hesitate to speak encouraging words
To hear what I must say

I yearn to find myself
This downfallen soul
Feel the creation
A fevered present
Hovering spirit of uncanny misery
Over my shoulder peering
I would never need any other as
I would call all the magic of the world
For loving ministrations to me

If I could find myself wandering
I would bring down the four columns
Of this world, slay
This creature
And bury and eat the fruits
That would grow from her
To feed the rest of my life

THE SECOND ANGEL PERSISTS IN SWEETER VOICE
Looking in her eyes, he sings:

All things seek self
In others, earth or sky

Neglected, lost and unborn self,
To heal, make whole
To play in celebratory joy
Love has won
Come be one

Maria replies:
One must sundered be
To touch, taste and see
That loss of one and all
Gives birth to self
In bitter grief

Grief feeds and loves
And cures the loss
In others, not binds,
To sameness tyranny

The angel, touching her, looks lovingly:
Grief cripples and blinds
To soft blandishments
But lips' sweet milk
And love's red marrow
Fills love's howl and void
Love has won
Come be one

Maria rejoins:
Joy possessed and hunger
Rends love's repose,
Verdant fields upturned
Are stripped by winds to sand
While joy released
As morning mist feeds

All creatures great and small
From love spawned

The angel breathes on her:
The clockwork of sun and moon
Measures eternity
Of tide and wind
The countless days
Of life's full stride
Through constant acts of love
Of all Earth's creatures locked
In ecstasy
Love has won
Come be one

Maria turns and in parting sings:
Though mind and word
Great chasms leap
And lust sweeps aside
Sweet mortality
The songbird's cries
Of love's kiss and sighs
Disperse in light and air
And our craft despairs
Of imitation
In echoes faint
Love has won
And now is gone

THE SECOND ANGEL SPEAKS AGAIN OF LOVE
The second angel accompanies himself
On a gourd-shaped lute:
Love red fog of whispering winds

Deep water through midnight ice
Burning words of loneliness
Showering from the sky

I am the one that loves you

Everyday windows in twisted shapes
Looking awry onto landscapes
Of lost desires, blossomed
Colors of every flower

I am the one

The white pelican dives
With pulled-back wings
The silvered fish slips to the foam
Let desire conjure flesh
Bring two selves to meet
To be forever the ones that love

I am

MARIA RESPONDS AGAIN TO LOVE
Across a distance she declaims:
What use romance
What is its weight in gold
A tree bears fruit, each different
And yet the same
Romance one taste
Then plants the seed
And burdens with
A lifetime of gardening,
Nursing, pruning care

If we be soul mates in purity
The only two which uniquely match
Support, complete the
Most essential spiritual selves
That through all destiny
And history, no other could
Aspire to, then let such spiritual majesty
Spiritual be, and I'll save
My pleasure for flesh-mate's delight

THE ANGEL, ANGRY, READIES TO DEPART
He throws his lute on the ground:
I dress myself in loving words
Purity of form and deeds,
I send my love as singing birds
To pleasure all your needs

Though all your foes would meet defeat
None greater than mine arm to virtue shield,
By force of threat and blood-splashed feats
Your eyes are stone, your heart won't yield

Thou foul creature, an asp, a thorn
A poisoned nettle gives relief
Would free me from a careworn
Life, joined to you in grief

MARIA'S REPLY
Until you gather the stars as sand
In plaited bins of lightning bolts
Not word, not loving look, nor deed
Will bear you fruit from seed

GUARIONEX
When all was done
Flesh was granted me
To complete this task as scribe
Inertia holds the world in place
Enslaved to its own path
Without destiny and out of sight
Of the One Supreme
Maria breaks these chains
To bring woman's reality

Angels of our fertile minds
Cloaked in flowered fields
Perfume our thoughts of self
Entice all portals of humankind
Childhood flavors, wants and needs
Bakeries of sweet bread and cakes
Air-whipped sugared cream
Music slipping through
Mountain scenes, lifting them
To air-brushed blissful dreams
Of paradise,

Angels of our fertile minds find
The bitter mutant rage of loss,
And cruelty endured,
Releasing, disguising it as gently gliding
Gulls on sea-sweeping winds,
Pretending presence of the One Supreme's
Reign in love and peace
Cleansing evil of gold and might
Deceiving love, action and purity
To serve betrayal and greed

You are not welcome here
My strength is righteousness
From the one who placed me here

Now Maria is my own
To guide and bring to love and self
For I have been granted shape
And substance too
She sleeps today's eternal sleep
Dream-swathed in selves of mighty deeds
A pleasured life, ownership,
Personas honed to conformity
To live long healthy lives
Inured from want, neighbors' depravity,
Mishap of luck, nutritional impulsivity
With minimal tithe in grace of God
To be among the lucky few that slip
Unknowingly to lifeless void

Wake now to other dreams,
For sleep and dreams will be
Your fate until you slip away
Like me to other lands
To observe, to guide and love,
Those in form and flesh
That wake to light and love

The One Supreme bests the beast
In every way to surpass the lure
Of Australian men, what best appearance
Brown of skin, manly dancer's grace
And sweet note lilt of musical voice,
And long-necked lute used by
The beast to sway to sin

But lending more readily to salvation's grace
As does this weak and foolish reed,
Humankind,

Hear Caribbean man's proudful lure
To give me shape,
What woman would not be drawn
By my every step, and soft songs of love
That written words cannot convey
But readers' imagination may supply
And will not fail to charm

Awake today to birthright dreams
Yours by grace of breath and sight
That love's purity be first of
One Supreme's creation, and not the
Mortal stuff of self, the beast's lure and net,
My eyes will serve your womanhood
As mirrors to your dreams
Do not bend to others' dreams
Of enslavement and base attainment
Cast aside proscriptions of ancient gods
Do not dismay nature's defoliation
Nor dream of self's commodities
Nor dance in metered time
Of pragmatic helpmate roles,
Concrete spires, art or philosophy
But be a god, your truest nature be
Not alone, in spite or fear,
But dance your wildest dance with me
That brings the heavens
Crashing down and up again

GUARIONEX, STRUMMING THE LUTE, SPEAKS TO MARIA
Awake
Wake not to dreams
Of golden aspirations
Spiraling ladders each step a goal
Each friend a helpmate bridge
To some place else
Each day a ship powered by winds of trade
Each place to birth exchange of esteem
And love designed for service
Trade and management

Wake now to dreams of me
The wind will catch your glide
Along the crystal neck
Of a mounting wave
In step the silvered fish flows
Behind the breaking head
Be still with me, the Earth revolves below
The wave must fall though suspended still
Don't call your name nor mine
For we would have to call
The name of everything
There is no name for goals
Of destiny, but deeds
That will bring the end

MARIA WAKES AND SEES GUARIONEX
Maria says,
"Though dressed in humble, homespun clothes
In angelic form surpassing the ones before

I sense no harm in you
But pleasing familiarity
In love and trust united
Closer, come speak to me"

Guarionex responds:
"Among the humors of your sleep
And warmth, your sweet moistures
From every portal rising
As swaying serpents seeking rest
And nourishment in the memories
Of all I have ever loved
I'll soon reveal to you my desire
To stand by your quest
As Guarionex with humming lute
And love to light your way
Fall down with me to an ancient land
Through the Earth's mantle
Of ancient ocean beds of coral rocks
To the center where it all began
With the first man laboriously
Starting his trek toward the light
And finding womankind
To bless his dreams"

THEY FELL FOR DAYS
Through many levels
Entwined in sheer delight
Of purity of two souls in joining embrace,
Through granite schist and great domed caves
They fell as air sweeps over the grass and plains
And faster still they fell, through shale and crystal

Through ancient coral beds and sand
And broke again through great domed rooms
Splintering water soaked encrusted walls
And floors, stalag mites and tites,
Into a colored rain of rock and spray
Through black cold lakes full
Of radiant yellow-green shrimps and fish
They fell as fireflies in flight
Into hidden rivers, deeper domes

Oblivious to time and pain they fell
As easily as sun's rays cleave the world
And as gently as the moon's glow silvers
The hollows of a lover's body, entwined
They fell as one, but not alone
At times in their downward fall
A creature seemed to pull away
From them and then rejoin,
A silhouette, a goat, a horse, a hirsute man
A beast seemed joined to them
A trick of the dark and spinning fall

And Guarionex said, we go to where it all began
He thought to his ancient land
But it was not to be, but a place
Much deeper still, and they ended
The fall on deep soft sand
Their destinies splayed, rent apart
Guarionex's desire his ancient home
Buried under aeon's neglect
Shunned by living things, except
The fallen leaves, a compost heap
Of dead and dying things, the sea

Still swayed, swelled and crashed
Impelled by winds from Africa,
The spray shattering upon the cliffs,
But sea nor rock overcame, in calm or fury
No advance made, awaiting Guarionex's
In full sway return from man to god

He took her hand to leave the caves
Behind, I will not stay but climb to light
As preordained, the beast has clung to us
Swerved and changed our course
To bury here our quest, ignore
The ancient god who speaks

THE THIRD ANGEL WHISPERS TO MARIA BUT NOT SO GUARIONEX MAY HEAR

You have come straight down
Many levels traversed
To return the path is too serpentine
So full of doubt, self-evaluation,
Human estimation of thought and deed
And consequence that to find
True direction or light of day
Will escape the cleverest prediction
Requiring such balanced knowledge
Of value and truth, deceit and ill-intention,
That one may only swerve from
Exertion, to invention to misdirection
The path from here only a god
Or god-directed may find
And then is so eternally long that all
Intention, thought and deed would fade
And fall on other creation

I await to bring light to all
Those born to this ancient land
That would incarnate
The One Supreme's intention

MARIA SPEAKS OF FREEDOM

Free of all, I would not love
Nor nurture, nor daughter, wife,
Nor partner, mother, but woman be
A spirit infusing all flying things
All beasts and man to be like me
To spawn loving things,
Born of music before the words
Each note creating synaptic fire shapes,
Constructed things of themselves
And others echoing in the mist,
Music and song that spawns
The birds, fruit and spices
The sighs to move the winds
And acrid smell of birth's blood
Around the world
That is my call that all things
Must pass through me
To see what they must be
Create these things
In formless void contained,
Clamoring, fertilizing each
And then the words to form the rocks and earth
Divide the land, sea and sky
Keep night from day
And name the sun and moon
And crown all with sprinkled
Sugar skulls beaming down as stars

To remind that humankind,
Given all, enslaves, destroys
The most precious womankind

GUARIONEX WARNS MARIA
Here is your ancient god
Disguised as youth to seduce
Chained by fate to foil his plans

THE ANGEL SPEAKS OF ALL, BEFORE TIME
There was no time, no meaning, memory
No recall, all was in all and all was all
All stood for one, and was one
And one stood for all, and was all
At reach, at hand, at thought, at sight
The One Supreme was all
To know the space of this
The time of this, we would be crushed
For in the all, only the One Supreme
Has thought, or reach, existence
No symbol, word or thought may follow
Upon another, for all follows all
No sequence, cause-effect, no word, no speech
No action, intent may cohere

But an impossibility circled,
A gleaming crystal against the dark
Of all, around the uncircumnavigable
Expanse of all,
The word the One Supreme
Would never say as long as all would be
Many and all ways, all things at once

All formful things,
Living and spiritual things
Thoughts and words and deeds
Were in all time, eternity,
Space, form, meaning were all in all

All did not move but stirred
As a cat might purr
Or a still pond might heave and pull
To the warming day and cooling night
This had always been, was and will be
Until a silvered darting thought
In the void, at the furthest
Margins of all, burst into all
In an unsustainable rounding flight,
A word, one word, *fini*

Time began, one instant different from all
That had gone before and the next
From difference grew memory
And there arose its twin, meaning,
And freedom and free will, and thus
The thought of humankind arose in ecstasy
And ended in regret with the One Supreme's
Abandonment of this earth, but leaving
Behind a gestating embryo god
Whose time has nearly come
To claim birthright and rule in love

The One Supreme stepped away from all
Though still being all, and divided every thing
From other things except the One Supreme
The end was wrought along with its
Gestation twin, the beginning,

This burst as light against the dark
And wrenched the heavens
Apart against the Earth,
The sun and moon were
Accidental sparks of a mighty cleaving blow
And a vibrating, startling snap
Of the One Supreme's coat of all
Sent the galaxies to disperse
And all was no longer in
The One Supreme
Though the One Supreme
Was still in All
And this caused life to blossom
In all profusive forms, uncountable,
Defining beauty and love even through
The paths that lead to malformed, evil, strange
And woman became the portal path
Of all

THE ANGEL SPEAKS OF THE GESTATING GOD AS MARIA STEPS AWAY WITH GUARIONEX

Maria hesitate, but hear of this god
That you must bear:
Those that sin come from him
His thoughts, missteps, desires
He must save them, even first,
To heal the world and himself, for he takes
Responsibility for all sin and all good
How can sin arise from
Perfect form, intention,
Immortality with no flesh to tempt
For creation unfettered to grow

To eternity, to explode from nothing
To heat and dust
All matter, force and energy
Inorganicity, to living observing beings
Able to give a name to the One Supreme
All matter force and energy must freely
Merge, emerge combine without precedence
Or thought to outcome, good or evil,
But always toward light and life
In awful multiplicity

THE THIRD ANGEL AS MARIA ASCENDS BEHIND GUARIONEX

I am not the ancient god
But unfairly chained to this rock
For love of humankind,
The embryo god bids me speak
To the vessel of the One Supreme's intent,
Approach and stay, these shackles loose
With your approaching step
I am the third angel of which Guarionex
Forewarned, but by the guile of
The One Supreme, I am in place now
Of the third evil beast that lures of might
And love would have foresworn

He would have talked of self
In such cunning ways that each time
You would have proclaimed authenticity
You would have betrayed yourself,
Each time you grasped essential
True-valued self, only greed

And duplicity would awaken,
He would have led to tranquil scenes
Of fulsome peace with hidden roots
In greed and misery, as none today
Escape his sophistry

Maria, I now am free
Descend with me to fire and heat
The explosive heart of this infant world
In squalling birth with outstretched limbs
And half-opened eyes to blurred blue sky
And sailing mountain clouds

Die if you must in my dark embrace
No loss in your aged despair
Ruminating of self-regard and rot
Creation's first thought is yet to come
And you will walk the Earth again
For all that lives must pass through you
In purity

All the gods will rise, greed the god,
And gluttony and gold, all those
Most worshiped by humankind
The giants and four winds, all gods
Shunned and slain, by humankind
In infancy, to give homage to
The seed of the One Supreme
In Earth's star-fire center being wrought,
A soul so great that only love emanates
And in which all our flesh-born deeds
Melt, recede to nothingness

MARIA ANSWERS THE THIRD ANGEL
Life perdurable
Leaps from husks
To stick and stone
Makes dance
From life within and song
And music too

Life remains though
The vessel dies
And you
But no catastrophe make
Of subject's introspective
Vanity

Life remains
Lion bits of fire scraps
That leap to Earth in light
And incend the plains

Life remains
As detritus silt of flesh
That buries the living
And twists, distorts it to
Shadowed aqueous hulks
Winged leviathans and
Crawling walking things
In choir songs
Of living joy
That pass to other shapes

I go with you,
I stay for the gestating god

That will wipe away
This grand mistake of love and sin redeemed
Born of this world, this god
Seeded by the One Supreme
Upon departure to leave us to
Our own devise

MARIA REMEMBERS A TROUBLED DREAM
What is this thing inside?
It kicks and moves
A moving shadow on the wall
Secret tapping on the floor
Come in or out
A message from before the light
A passage trembling in the womb
From before to now to then
To future dreams
And I in swollen prime
A sweet ripe fruit
Let me eat the world
To give this thing
Its wings, fly free
Not weighed down by need
Or brought to practicality
So I may ravish it with
My eyes and thoughts of love

I am summoned now to angelic strength
By the procreative universe
Come stars, sun, moon, Earth,
Sea, great hurricanes and tides,
One Supreme, aid this fleshy

Pain-wracked vessel in throes
Of birth's banal miracle
Shield me from dreams of
Child's divinity and humankind's
Striving to paradise
But grant me gentle sleep
In the unbroken flow of flesh
And awakening to the wails
Of a newborn hungry child
That must speak
In woman's words

MARIA SINGS TO GUARIONEX
Don't stop nor turn,
My footsteps fall in time to yours
That's why they are not heard
I'll sing and by my voice you will
Know I follow
Precede, announce, prepare
The ground for me

The night-dressed moon
The light-blazed sun
The turning flower
The pollen-dusted bee
The lion and the lamb
The sea-born man
And city woman say
Marry me, marry me

They fear it will never be
It will never be

The night flees
The fire of the sun
The day extends to
It will never be
I live in Soledad
Where night quenches the sun
Yearning for never be
Never be

Whispered words of bees,
The wind brushes by,
Guarionex, I hear
I turn and you are gone,
My hand grasps the air
I walk in Soledad

You were and I
It will never be
I sing it will never be
Soledad is sweet and suckles me

I will not die
Death is the end of all
It will never be, never be
Precede, prepare for me

GUARIONEX IN SORROW ASKS
Sing of love a happy song
Before we reach the light

Maria sings:
If we could fly

We'd soar the sky
Full of joy
We'd part and join
Never destroy our love
Its force will ride
The tide and winds
And lift our souls
Beyond the cries
Of bodies' lust
To perch on gates
Of heaven's walls
And rain our notes
As comet's tears
On the fiery pain
And hellish fears
Of those below

GUARIONEX ARRIVES ALONE AT HIS ANCIENT HOME
He turns, looks back
To the bowels of the Earth, and says,

Realizing he's alone
By the carving inscribed "*amador*":

"The blue-green current
Of the sea
Slips to the steel ice-black depths
Where once living
Things silt down to fill
The rifts of drowned volcanoes
The lap of gods receiving lives

Dreamt in futility"

"How may I love again
But to swallow the deep
And disgorge laughter
That moves the moon
From its firmament
And wakes the pulse of wave
And tide"

"To surround,
Draw you down
From heaven's throne
To my embrace"

GUARIONEX'S LAST WORDS
Debased, displaced by fate's
Cruelties and neglect
With innocence and love
As love's last resort
It is pain, loss and madness
Which distort the soul
To refractive clarity
Shining from within an
Arced rainbow over heaven's gate

I take my place within a winged
Leviathan, sandstone rock carved
To shape by wind and tide
Throughout millenniums
To wait besides this carving of
This blessed mother for woman's return

Maria will live again and I will
Announce and protect her quest
To best the beast and bring to Earth
A holy time of union with
The One Supreme in All

UPON THAT LAND TODAY
In Guarionex's ancient home
The land of the sun
From whose mountains
The crimson sun in
Its downward course
Surrounds the Earth
In bands of many hues
And at which shore,
One may find revealed
A stone-encased ammonite shell,
Stands a winged leviathan besides
A queen with "*amador*" inscribed

They await creation's birth

BOOK 8

SORAIA

THE HUMBLE SCRIBE DREAMS OF SORAIA (ISLAND OF THE DEAD)

AWAKENING

The Earth broke as a great gourd
Splitting and spilling the seas and
Behemoths upon the land
I rode the waves naked of body,
Mind and thought, expelled in
Dizzy ecstasy to the swirling
Waters filling rocky rifts
And plains so only mountaintops
Were left exposed

Though fear and death were to be
Constant companions, a fierce
Living joy of each moment's infinity
Would meet their assail-- even their victory

This before all time, even as the Earth
And land became themselves, and as a surge
Carried me upended, toward an unfinished
Sky, blackened as the remnant of an eternal fire,
In the distance, small rocky specks,
Islands all, were spread in a great arc, as
The One Supreme may cast the seeds of
Destiny and humankind's suffering

This before all time, still in darkness,
Even as Guarionex, the first of the name,
Struggled to climb toward light's allure
I spied a spoor of what might be light
Which prompted me to open my eyes
For I had been witnessing my soul's
Dream of eternity, and only now
Fallen to life's embrace

This as time began its rhythmic beat,
From a cave the moon emerged
Clothed in modesty of clouds
As silvered gown and veils, announcing
In reflected light the stirring of the sun,
And as it crossed the blackened sky
It wrote in fiery signs and shapes, for
Humankind to decipher, the placement
Of the stars

As time achieved its promise
Of constancy, the sun emerged not
Far behind, not warning of its
Earthly dominance, and the oceans
Swirled as behemoth and all its kin
Emerged to bathe in life-giving warmth
And then dove to the coolest depths in fear
To allay the fears of all, the Sun
Promised a timely rise and set,
And constancy of warmth
Regardless of virtue, grace or interest

MEETING GUARIONEX, LAST OF THE NAME

The clouds wept for him in squalls of rain,
The wind ripped from him his pain and sighs
In rumbling moans and keening cries
Announcing them to the world
The wind lifted, roiled the surf to carve
The sand and rock to jagged shapes
Covered the land in a diaphanous veil
Of mist of salt and water

The sun broke through, forgot its gentleness
So much for promises
And withered all plant, animal and bird;
No respite from moon and stars
They covered all in hollowed silver shadows
Of stillness

The end had come, the passage of days complete
An eternal string of pearls, a pearl for every day
Unstrung, falling free, scattered into past time

Guarionex alone at the line where
Featureless sea meets a dense hard sky
All those he loved emerging from the past
And I to be at his side again

I drifted to a rocky shore and sleeping
Awoke as the morning sun pushed
Aside the Dawn who in her red
And golden gown chased the Night,
Now whom she loved but could never reach,

As a distant echo
I heard Guarionex's familiar call
But he was nowhere to be seen
The sun glided past midday's zenith
And started its seaward evening's fall
As I walked on the sandy arc where
Sea met the shore,

As evening's graying veil fell upon the world
And birds of every color announced
Their descent to evening's roost,

I saw him wave from atop a karst mound
So high I could not see his face
But his graceful form and voice
Called me forth

CAIBAI (CAVE OF THE DEAD)

The karst was crowned with the
Protuberant mouth of a cave
Which did not dare to enter, bat,
Swallow, nor iguana
I wove my steps around
A growth of dense spiked cactus
And left a trail of blood
Eternity veils me as carnate man
Bearing suffering of flesh and blood
In my earthly forays

Surrounding the opening of the cave
A grove of guananaba bushes grew
Their ripe fruit splayed upon the ground,
And their black seeds embedded in the
Pulpy white flesh looking at me
As the eyes of the dead

Guarionex laughed and said
The dead eat these when they wander
Out at night, come before night falls
And they venture forth
I was naked and so was he
As all the multitude of his people
Unashamedly walked, as only those free
Of the first sin may walk, now all dispersed

But mostly dead, cruelly slain though
Only with the weight of sins that those that are
Still children of the One Supreme may carry

With open kindness greeting the ships and
Tending with cleverness and patience
The awareness of the presence of
The One Supreme
Wardens of the gifts bestowed and
At the threshold of consciousness
Of the greater secrets of mastery
In a frenzy of gold and lust
Slain by those of the white bird ships
And lost to a world condemned to
Repeat such massacres even unto now
And forevermore,

The greatest of blasphemies,
To slay in the name of the One Supreme
Those still kept in the Garden of Paradise
Before they knew to sin

THE DESCENT
The limestone rock shaped to fluted edges
By rain and wind, tore at our feet, though
Toughened to thick pads of flesh, and soon
We both were leaving a trail of blood
That glowed in purple droplets
In the light of the rising moon

From deep beneath the earth there was
A wailing chorus cry, of a river's rushing

Waters, expelled sighs, a storm-preceding wind,
I could not tell, my steps stopped though
I willed them forward, Guarionex continued forward,
No word, no backward glance, I could see
The lengthening glowing purple trail

Now I willed my steps, though still frozen,
To stop, though eternal spirit, I live in
The grace of the One Supreme,
Yes, dear reader, the humble scribe
Who insults you and takes your cowardice
To task, fears the One Supreme, fears stepping
Outside the grace and presence of the One Supreme
I knew one more step would take me into
Another land, a different place, where only
Chaos reigned and the clockwork of reality
Even light and time are replaced by suffering
Guarionex, as always, drew me forward
To witness, record, relate the truth to all
If I could eat this bitter book of this
Small tale, I would and let it be told
At the end of all by someone else,
But Guarionex went on and so did I

We descended many years, through
Many nightmare dreams that I would
Ascribe to fantasy had I not traveled
Through history, to all the wars and riots
Of humankind, even to the first
Of brother slaying brother
And even to the last, dear reader,
When all you think permanent, bestowed
And sacred, is destroyed in willful
Revenge for an imagined slight,

All this, all the machinery, misplaced
Limbs and body parts, until arriving
At an Earth-encircling cavern hung
With luminous vines, and small
Barb-tailed scuttling scorpions
With sharp razor teeth, and these
Biting and devouring numberless
Of humankind, their tears of pain
And regret giving birth to a raging
Torrent coursing through the home
Of the dead,

The sentry, a prodigious sleeping bat,
Wakefulness unnecessary
For the captive hordes had well-formed
But useless arms and legs
The torrential cascades of cries of pain
Pleas for a final sleep, regret, the clarion
Sounds of seven trumpets each calling
For the din of martial horses and armored men
The clang of iron and steel, the smell
Of bridles, blankets, blood, the fearful
Braying of man and steed, forming
Phalanx of flesh and metal to kill
A portion of humankind

We walked among these masses
Dying many deaths, until we came
Upon the most pitiable, the most assailed
Justly so, the monks and chroniclers
The holy scribes who knew observed
And witnessed the cruelest slaughter
And torture of the innocents, even of
Infants, amputated, and run through

With spears, and yet called them
Of the ancient enemy while the holy
Scribes did the devil's work

Time is only of the mortal sphere
And circles round so the end of time
Touches the beginning, in Caibai
All time exists in the present
Infinity and all things exist
In the instant, Guarionex spoke
In a kindly way and asked,
"Did not Juan Pablo and Francisco too
Call your acts sin, and did not Bartolomé
Call it slaying of innocents, without cause,
Of those without sin?

And did you not think in the death and killing
Of Agueybana, of Urayoan, Coxiguez, Yauco,
Jumacao, Loquillo and many more hunted
And betrayed, that nothing was amiss
And that families would kill themselves
And their progeny rather than be enslaved
And nothing wrong with burning to death
In deceitful ambush a village of the most
Noble of humankind?"

"And you of Burgos, the Bishop, the slaughter
Of a thousand children and another thousand
And upon them even another thousand
That it was of no concern to you
The Vicar of Christ?"

*"And you, seeker of the eternal waters,
Did you not fear to live in eternal damnation?"*

*And Guarionex reproached each one
Of each sin to the innocents, and it took
One hundred years, and finally he said,
"Did you call yourselves holy while defiling
The Name of the One Supreme
The Same worshiped by these innocents
Of Paradise?"*

*"And so this book declares that your names will
Be forever lost to saying, learning and memory
And the names of the holy innocents
The children of the One Supreme
Forever remembered"*

*And there arose the greatest of dins
The clarion call of a thousand upon
A thousand horns each saying
The name of a thousand upon
A thousand upon a thousand
Names of the innocents who died
In the embrace and love of the One Supreme*

BOOK 9

THE FINAL WORDS

ESSENCE

Does the sun know its nature
Or remember its creation?
Is it the fury of eternal fire it apparents
Or the gassy brood it feeds and all
The creatures of its flowing mantle
Of substance that rise to worship at
The multiple dawns of all its spheres?

Is the comet its own creation
Of which it played no part?
Is it the icy collection of water and rock
Its streak through the universe or
The foreboding of omens, predictions
And justification of sins
It prompts throughout aeons?

Is the musician recipient of a gift
Of voice not of her intention or design
Nor worth? Does the rider or the steed
Shape the qualities, the highs, the lows
The pace of breath and stance? Does the
Rider care but for response, and the steed
Only for feeling's phrase?

These strange silvered shadows rising
From the deep, what benign hand
Fashioned them, what words declared
They would feed the world?
The fisherman is master of only
What he makes, the net, not the force
Of the One Supreme

Neither rider nor fisherman enters
The heart of what sustains them
The singer mishears the voice
So we who talk and act
And call us ourselves only are
Part of what we truly are
Which comes before we are named
And shapes both action and sight
But lasts and forever is a stranger
That passes through
Humanity indistinguishable
As brutish and divine for neither
Shows mercy born of compassion

THE ANCIENT ONE SPEAKS
The One Supreme is but a shadow
Seen through mist from the darting
Corners of our sight and may not be defined
But to serve as difference that leads
To war and brutality

I practice no grand design
No lurking evils, machinations
But freely receive sufficient
Unto each day the evil wrought
By humankind's proclivities

GUARIONEX, THE ARCHANGEL, SPEAKS UPON READING MCGOWAN, THE EXPECTED ONE:
"The greatest light attracts
the deepest darkness."

Great flaming bird, the One Supreme
Recalls my name and wakes me
Through your cries
Natural stance assumed
Before and after time exists
The round surround of eternity
Not measured in step on step
Nor mortared walls, but measures
Of light, fire, existence and meaning
Meaning not of inclusion, but
Including all, not in death
But nonexistence, now and forever,
For in eternity all exists
And identity belongs to mortality

But I am of this flow of things
A moveless blowing wind
A raging river that neither flows up or down
For eternity, all eternal things
Exist in stillness, silence
Pervading unendingly

Here I stand before and after
My Earth's sojourn in materiality,
Now a light
In the dark of eternity

BOOK 10

EPILOGUE I
VARIOUS POEMS POSTERIOR TO ETERNITY

A MINOR GOD POSTS ON FACEBOOK AFTER VISITING THE UPPER WEST SIDE, NYC

Let's roll Jupiter here
And there, red Mars;
A slingshot for Mercury
To burst the two apart

The flow of folk in red, blue
Yellow and green
Tightly tied Rockport postal shoes,
Teetering leopard-spotted heels high,
Horses and trams as corpuscles
Bringing flowing life to
The city's stirring limbs,
Absorbing life's force,
Discharging organs, productivity,
Centuries as fleeing shadows

Not even gods see the flowing force
Goals, future, past, dreams
Dreamt nor undreamt, intent
All ending before meaning is born

THE HUMBLE SCRIBE READS "MIXTURAO" BY TATO LAVIERA

Black Colossus striding continents
Of words in easy steps,
Beating Mixturao on drums, violins
Grunts and prayers
Sublime, abstract, above, floating free,

Not contained by the
Black gowns of university dons
Your thoughts woven of ethereal threads
Of spiritual passion and sight
And resounding with the heart's beat,
The blood's thrushing flow
You live in my step and speech
And whisper still of secrets
Beyond my ken

Freedom not endowed, nor lost,
But in the walk and talk,
Though sweetly dreaming
Even in a bitter world,
Your words still swagger
With your voice singing songs
Each word an actor upon a stage
With character, will and wisdom
Wielding a sword that gives life to truth
They speak of you, your thought
And world, your love of all
Your words use us as your voice

EPILOGUE II

THE ONE SUPREME'S REGRETS
This wondrous blue-domed world
Explodes in colored blossoms
And down below, in lightless rock-framed nests
Crystal gems expand to meters
That click, one life a beat, and aeons pass
From seed to hollow orbs
Whose heavens of ruby red
Purple, green, or icy gleam
Shine as countless fire galaxies
Distant from our grasp
In buried earth of deep-inverted
Mountain ranges that mirror
The riotous spring of tender sprouts
And fragrant green and colors
Of all living things, yearning and desire
The claw but also the teat

In motion set against these striving things
That need but air and sun and gentle rain
That still stand strong against nature's
Most ravaging storms
And twist and turn, survive,
Change in time to drought and flood
And spring as colored arcs from every leaf,
Set against these children of eternal spring
Of my eye and flowing breath
From the spinning stars in their teeming nurseries
Is not god, magic hand of Lucifer, nor fate
Nor inevitability
But humankind.

ONE SUPREME'S LAMENT UPON LEAVING HUMANKIND

White corpuscles and red I shaped to live in harmony,
One ferocious to lie in wait to spring to your defense,
The other humbly serving all of which you are composed.
Legions of living things I swooped from Earth and sky
Even dust from the canopied void, unseen and small,
But in their numbers shape your shadow and its gait.
One word, no more, and each took up infinite toil,
To serve in diverse rapport your destiny.
Have I not said, first will the humblest be
And yet these you disdain and use to extinguishment,
The wondrous air refreshed by wind and rain
These mechanics of my world,
The forest whispers, the moon and tides,
You made to gods, worshiped them and abandoned me,
But soon to disdain, betray and them destroy

Upon the pregnant Earth's full bounty, I gave you birth,
The smallest of my creatures digesting rock
And sand to fertile earth, and grass and fruited plains
And the creatures that live upon the world
Your crib mates in shape and heart, fear of night,
And love of running upon the vast expanse
Caressed by wind and sun and moon's glow
The furred and furless, and feathered ones, all
Did you not see their beauty which I made
To humble you, remind of my word and hand,
It is the humble I love the most,
But you have filled with pride
Though all was given and all you had to do
Was take and take you did as though
Creation was your most despised self

To be owned and destroyed, but you are it's creature
And not the reverse.

I honeyed with joyful delight essential human needs:
Pure water, the flowing crystal form of the stars,
To quench your thirst, not dull surfeit, but cool
And full satisfaction that fills with life,
Clears the eyes of film, and brightens to glow of day
Life's desire and frees the mind to expansive thought
And hunger sated not with abecedary algorithms of scientific words
But quiet longing, calm respite of fretted dread and the balm of sleep
And continued life, offspring, no need to go beyond imperative drive,
But I bestowed it with pleasure full to find the other
In open and boundless love in joyful union
Even as I love you.

I toil for you as the wind with transparent hand
Eviscerates the bowels of the Earth,
Forms fluted mountain shapes, bends trees to its form,
Spurs the salted waves white foam to tendrils
That shape the land and carve the rocks
And slowly melt the face of Time.
The wind carves the clouds to parodies of shapes
And punctures them for sun's release in crimson sheets
And to reflect moon's pallor glow
With color I endowed the fields.
The flower's hue is not for aggrandizement
But man's spiritual wonder and the bird and insect's thrill
And to contain my word,
Yet all serves your pride and its own swelling.
I spoke not for your sake but for love,
My word brings forth all things that on
Your heart impinge.

From mote of dust unseen for eternity
I drew forth light, form and flesh.
With one word whose utterance is not yet done
Creation's work is just begun.
Light will yet rage and fire too
With keening cries that liquefy
Galaxy strings of sparkling fuses
Ending in universal flames and giving rise
To profligate creations in nooks and crannies
Of Time that holds in place the warp and woof
Of myriad universes falling as snowflakes
Intermixed as the differing hues of one flower's petal
Not hidden from each, not impinging.

How does spirit, extinguished by faithlessness and loss,
Fly from ash to fire born?
A thunderbolt, capricious thrown by laughing Jove,
Or born by thought and reason finding the way of an inner maze
Great machines to dig your inner womb.
What is humankind without the tools of thought and steel
But spirit pure, a soul debased by effort
Lost in the act of finding the way
Will thought or reason spool the way
Find tools to measure and maps to plot the course
Levers of words to parse your past mistakes?

Carnal lust, orgasmic reflex, but one first step
To lead to love of other not self nor self's release
Wandering lost in conundrums of relationship
Not to thrill but give one's self to other
Devoid of self, present to lover's will,
To lose boundlessly incoherently

To receive the other in place of self
Create a new self, personhood of two.

To search consciousness and truth, I set you free
Though I would have preferred to keep you
In my embrace, unharmed by sinful greed
But not freedom, nor greatness's quest you sought
But cruel blind acts so vile that they
Outweigh all the poisoned detritus that you
Have given as food and air to all that lives.
You look upon this calamity and call for the end of time
You think your sins, misuse of all
Augur Armageddon, the end of all
And my kindly and infinite rule
And hold me to the words that
Tribulations announce the end of time
Unrolling over blooded detritus of your own kind
You have lost the mute herd bliss
Feeding on grass in eternal todays
And the innocence of the lion eating its prey.
Knowledge has made you criminals of your own nature
Condemned to suffer at your own hand.
Now you think that these acts so vile
Augur pain's surcease
No regret, no repair but force my hand to end your pain
But no end will fall from acts of hands of man,
But mine.
I shall cut into this gourd of a planet
As my terrible sweet angels that make instruments
Of hollowed orbs, pull filaments of light across the dark spaces
And pluck notes which evanesce into forms much like you
Crying and dancing through the reaches of time's sorrows

Wondrous creations that make songs
Of rock, deep caves, blue sky and roiling sea
Whose nascent force to love create leaping edifices
Of thought illuminating the inner chambers of matter,
Life and the blurred spaces starlit by my falling words.

Suffer and wait
For only spirit will bring the end
That echoes the Creator's acts
If there be but one that loves the world as I and joins
The winged sparrows' calls of sorrow
In their fall at hands of humankind
I will send my Seed to you.